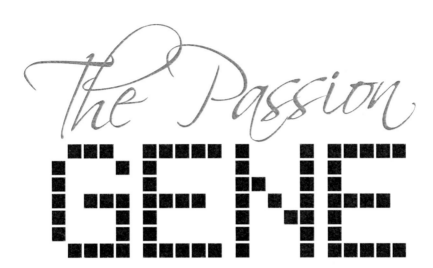

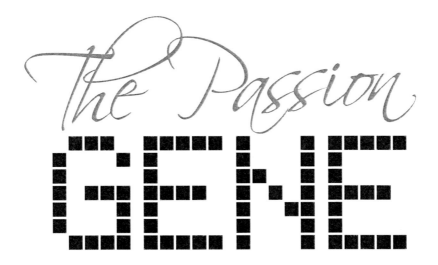

The Passion GENE

MEMOIRS
Cirencester

Published by Memoirs

MEMOIRS
PUBLISHING

Memoirs Books

25 Market Place, Cirencester, Gloucestershire, GL7 2NX
info@memoirsbooks.co.uk www.memoirspublishing.com

Copyright ©Louis De Savy, February 2012
First published in England, February 2012
Book jacket design Ray Lipscombe

Printed in England

ISBN 978-1-908223-75-3

From the wreck of the past, which hath perish'd,
Thus much I at least may recall,
It hath taught me that what I most cherished
Deserved to be **dearest of all:**
In the desert a fountain is springing,
In the wild waste there is still a tree,
And a bird in the solitude is singing
Which speaks to my spirit of Thee.

Lord Byron.

Mon âme a son secret, ma vie a son mystère:
Un amour eternel en un moment conçu,
Le mal est sans espoir, aussi j'ai dû le taire,
Et celle qui l'a fait n'en a jamais rien su.

Félix Anvers.

CONTENTS

CHAPTER ONE

Georgiana had an abiding, irrational phobia. She always dreaded the thought of missing a flight and saw to it that she arrived at an airport a good two hours in advance. This was how it always was with her.

If she were going on holiday, the time was spent enjoying a drink or a meal and reading those columns of her daily newspaper which she usually ignored because she could not afford the time to indulge in trivia. Idleness was not part of her philosophy. She thrived on being unfalteringly active.

If she were on her way to a scientific meeting, the time would usually be devoted to catching up with as-yet unread articles, or more frequently to tapping at her laptop, treasuring the cherished hoards of information it held. She had other reasons for arriving early on such occasions: she could book herself into a non-smoking area on the plane and, most important for her, get a window seat.

On that second Tuesday of a warm August she was due to catch the 17.55 from London Heathrow to Helsinki for a two-day meeting scheduled for early on the Thursday morning. It would have been too risky trying to catch the Wednesday afternoon plane, in case she missed it. Early that morning she had gathered together all the accoutrements she was planning to take with her to Finland.

'Are you going to take your usual containerload or are you travelling light for a change?' asked Philip, her husband, with an indulgent smile.

'A woman needs to take as much as she can' she retorted. 'Even if she is not going to use it all.'

She enjoyed dressing well, the more so since she could afford it.

'I suggest you travel light. You won't have time to wear all this' he replied, pointing at the clothes heaped up on the bed. But Georgiana was not prepared to be nagged. She decided to mark time until he left the house for work.

'Have a good time' he said, giving her a parting kiss.

'Chance would be a fine thing' was her reply. 'You know conferences nowadays, you barely have time to breathe.'

She saw him to the front door and he waved her goodbye as he drove off. She thought about his remark about her luggage. He was quite right.

Back in the bedroom, she decided to be more discriminating. She would travel light for a change, piling everything into her elegant but capacious Dior holdall. She would halve the formal wear and take only a selection of the sensual lingerie that she loved wearing for the pleasure it gave her.

'I'll put some of my classical tapes in' she muttered to herself. 'Must remember to jot down the hotel phone number.'

She left Bath just after 1.30 pm in a buoyant mood. It was her first opportunity to give a seminal talk at a meeting where most of the other speakers would be men or women of distinction. It was a daunting thought, but equally so it was one that elated her. She saw this as the peak of her career so far. For the past two years working as a research fellow, she had been absorbed in the scientific aspects of an advanced therapeutic project in Ken Taylor's medical unit, and her researches were to form the nucleus of a PhD thesis.

It was not merely a turn of the wheel of fortune. There was more to it than just chance, which is rarely unprompted. She knew that it was the privilege of those who toil to be in the right place at the right moment. Deep inside, Georgiana felt that the tide was now flowing for her.

Ken had been invited by Satra, a Scandinavian drug house, to give an important communication on a breakthrough venture of theirs on forward-looking DNA therapy. Georgiana had done most of the work for the talk and would have accompanied him as his colleague. However, on the Thursday evening a new consultant cardiologist was being appointed to work in tandem with Ken's unit. As he was also the senior figure in the Department of Medicine he had to be present at the selection committee, all the more so since it was for the choice of a colleague who would be working close to him.

The date could not be altered, and suddenly Georgiana was catapulted into the lecturer's seat. She had already proved herself equal to such tasks and Ken had no hesitation in sending her in his place. For her, as a young scientist, this was a matter for real pride. She was able to share it with her husband, who was head of research and development for a specialised branch of a local pharmaceutical company.

Georgiana was more anxious than usual to arrive on time, preferably a day in advance. She had never been to Helsinki and wanted to take the opportunity to see the city. Her Saturday afternoon was already booked for a satellite working session with international colleagues who were involved in similar studies, so she had booked her return flight for the Sunday afternoon.

She preferred to drive her Toyota Celica to the airport rather than travel tediously via Reading or Slough by train. She enjoyed listening to classical music in the car. It helped that a male cousin of hers managed one of the local airport hotels and could offer her a free parking space and the benefit of the courtesy coach to the various terminals. Everything had come together to work in her favour. Luck really seemed to be going her way.

She enjoyed dressing well, even when travelling. She decided to put on her elegant but comfortable green trouser suit, which she could also wear for touring.

Georgiana had driven down the A46 to junction 18 of the M4 and then on down the motorway to London so many times that she knew all the signs and service stations by heart. Though she had seen the landscape at all seasons and in all weathers, she never tired of it. Nature held a Wordsworthian fascination for her. Studying it complemented the scientific side of her nature, perhaps because both aspects are born out of the ability to observe.

The A46 offers little to the traveller and can be woefully slow, thanks to the many heavy lorries making their way to the M4. A car radio is a blessing. As she left the city behind her and headed out into the late summer countryside she turned on Radio 4 to catch the end of The World at One and listen to The Archers, to which she was addicted. The road was fairly clear and she found herself speeding along the escarpment. Below her in the valley to the west she glimpsed the gentle green folds of Dyrham Park.

She joined the M4 at precisely two o'clock; plenty of time to spare. The hourly news was dominated by the various embargoes imposed by the United Nations on Iraq for its unwelcome invasion of Kuwait. She reached for a cassette she had bought a few days previously with the intention of listening to it on the journey, and clicked it into the Celica's radio. It was Tasmin Little's interpretation of Max Bruch's Violin Concerto. She loved the imaginative quality of Little's virtuoso.

Junction 18 stands on the crest of the southernmost extremity of the Cotswold Hills. From here, when darkness falls, one can see to the west the myriad lights of Bristol scintillating like a golden Milky Way. To the east, the motorway descends into Wiltshire through the Vale of Malmesbury with its lush pasture and arable land and then across the River Avon to the first services at Leigh Delamere. The undulating Marlborough Downs fill the landscape with their verdant slopes. On that afternoon, under a clear blue sky, they were like a painter's palette brushed with exploratory shades of green.

CHAPTER ONE

This stretch of the country lies over the Jurassic belt of limestone and clay which sweeps from the Cotswolds through Oxford and from there all the way to the Wash. Beyond Swindon, between the Berkshire and Marlborough Downs, the motorway has hewn a path through a bed of limestone which exposes its many strata as if to remind the speeding traveller of the slow pace of geological time.

The combine harvesters had clearly been at work. In the fields to the left were stacked rectangular bales of straw, while on the right, rolled bundles in their black plastic wraps were dotted all over the mown fields. On the meadows between these fields and the road, herds of indolent cows were grazing unperturbed by the passing cars. Black and white Friesians intermingled happily with brown Herefords with their off-white faces and aprons, or side by side with Dairy Shorthorns in their pale reddish and white livery. It was a tranquil world not troubled by discrimination of colour or breed.

As Georgiana passed the signpost to Bowood House the music swelled into the haunting tenderness of the end of the first movement as it blended into the second. She had visited Bowood many times. It was here, almost a century before Bruch had composed his concerto, that Joseph Priestley had discovered oxygen. Both men were part of her culture, the one for her love of music, the other for her scientific education. To her, science and art were both forms of communication which used the same pathway of comprehension to bring to the notice of onlookers what the scientist or the artist had observed; the one to appeal to the soul, the other to cast light on the unexplained. She felt conscious of her advantaged background, cradled in affluence. The words of Alexander Pope flashed through her mind:

CHAPTER ONE

Lo, the poor Indian! whose untutored mind
Sees God in clouds, or hears him in the wind;
His soul proud Science never taught to stray
Far as the solar walk or milky way;
Yet simple Nature to his hope has given,
Below the cloud-topped hill, an humble heaven.

As she sped past Swindon the music was building to a crescendo. The flatter countryside was now replaced by a mammiliform scenery of verdurous mounds on which yet more cattle grazed. Here, in the very early morning, the low eastern sun would silhouette their shapes over the ridge of these hillocks, while in late spring the ploughs would churn up the limestone subsoil along narrow stretches as if they were chalky white runners unfurled over a vast green carpet.

Soon she saw the tall radio mast that told her she was approaching Berkshire and was over halfway to the airport. She would be there in good time. As she passed Membury, the concerto had reached its finale and then only the soft sound of the tyres on the road filled the car. She reached blindly for another cassette, ejected Bruch's, slid the new one in and found she had selected Beethoven's Ninth. The traffic was still flowing freely as she passed Junction 14.

Shortly afterwards, the speed indicator in the centre reservation began flashing '50'. 'Bother' she said to herself. She took her foot off the accelerator and moved to the inside lane. Within a mile she had ground to a halt, while the traffic in the other lanes was barely moving. Ahead she could see a long snake of cars, three wide, winding all the way up the hill and beyond.

Georgiana's previously joyous mood changed to one of indignation. 'Why the hell don't the fools give warning before the junction rather than after it?' she thought to herself. She could have left the motorway and gone through Hungerford and Newbury. But it was too late, and now she was trapped in an inescapable standstill.

Soon drivers began to climb out of their cars and pace about on the silent carriageway, chatting to each other. She decided to do the same - perhaps someone would be able to tell her the reason for the jam. But no one could. One of the drivers was trying to call the AA on his new mobile telephone, but the line was constantly engaged.

A depressing hour passed before the news came that a lorry stacked with bales of straw had overturned and discharged its load over the cars in the two other lanes, causing the inevitable pile-up.

Georgiana was lost for a moment. Then it occurred to her that she might be able to take advantage of being in the nearside lane to chance driving on the hard shoulder to Junction 13, which she knew must be less than three miles away. It would be an act of delinquency, but it had to be weighed against the horror of missing her flight. She knew that on one of the 'Works Unit Only' side roads the police often lay in wait, and the risk was too great.

Soon it was past four o'clock. There was a real danger that she would not get to Heathrow on time. She was still an hour from the airport, on top of the time she would need to park her car.

As she stood on the hard shoulder, the blue flashing lights of a police car appeared a hundred yards or so away down the hard shoulder. Without thinking it through, she stepped forward and put up her hand. To her amazement the car stopped.

'What's the problem, madam?' said the driver.

'I'm very sorry for being so presumptuous' she said. 'I'm desperate to get to London Airport to catch a flight to an important medical meeting. Can I please drive on the hard shoulder to the A34? I know the route to the airport from there.'

The two police officers conferred for a minute or so, Georgiana tactfully moving away from the window. 'You'd better drive in front of us, madam' the driver said. 'Otherwise we could start a mad rush.'

'You are angels!' she exclaimed with a smile of relief, not forgetting a winsome twinkle. 'Is it clear beyond Junction 12?'

'Yes, madam. The accident is about three miles west' replied the policeman.

Georgiana jumped into her car and the police car backed for a few yards to let her through. As she left the motorway, she waved to them and they responded by flashing their headlights.

After turning off at Junction 13, she drove into Chieveley service station and called her cousin's hotel.

'The Heathrow Royal. This is Sarah' answered the telephonist. 'How can I help?'

'Can you put me through to the manager please? It's urgent. Tell him it's his cousin.'

Bland music clicked in as she waited - one of those inventions of industrial psychologists who imagine that pleasant sounds will soothe away the irritation of waiting. Fortunately, it soon stopped.

'John here. Where are you, Georgie?'

'I've been stuck in a traffic jam. I'm ringing from Chieveley. I'm going to be late. Will you be able to drive me to Terminal 1 when I get to the hotel?' she asked.

'Why don't you just drive straight there?' replied John. 'I'll take the courtesy coach now and meet you at the pick-up point to collect your car. It'll be a lot quicker.'

'Good thinking. See you there. Many thanks.'

She put back the receiver and rushed back to her car. There was some traffic through Newbury, but she lost no time on the A4 and rejoined the motorway at Junction 12. She got to Heathrow just before half past five, thanking her stars that she had taken her husband's advice. Her cousin had already told the British Airways desk of her delay. She hugged him and rushed into the terminal, making straight for the departure gate.

CHAPTER TWO

Robin Chesham had also been invited to speak at the conference. Though the mapping of the human genome was still some 10 years away, Satra was already thinking 15 years ahead, and it had started a project that could selectively detect faulty DNA and thereby offer individual treatment. Such gene therapy would be the future of medicine, for hand-picked cases. This was what had attracted Robin to the project he had joined.

As a surgeon on the staff of the General, he was highly organised. He had rooms in Devonshire Place where he would consult on a Wednesday morning. He could walk from there to the nearby independent hospitals to operate in the afternoon.

Robin had arrived at Terminal 1 accompanied by his secretary Margaret, who was to take his car back. He always travelled light to avoid booking queues or having to wait for his luggage on his return. To make up for the time he often spent out of the country at scientific meetings, he ran his life on a tight schedule. After his appointment as a consultant he had reorganised his timetable so that his Wednesdays were always his own. During the ascendant years of his junior career he had learned from his seniors that it paid to take a whole day off in the middle of the week. He also knew that it was a peculiarity of his profession that scientific meetings were all too frequently held on a Friday, so he had seen to it that his own free time did not fall on that day.

The gate number of the flight was already on the flight screen, so he made his way quickly to the Executive Club to book his seat and thence to the departure lounge. On the way he called in at the duty-free shop, where a half-bottle of vintage Veuve Clicquot attracted his attention. He was not likely to find such a thing in Helsinki, but he was quite prepared to take it all the way back if necessary. Anyway, he would not have to carry anything far as he would be picked up on his return on the Sunday by the ever-devoted Margaret.

He spoiled himself, but felt he had worked hard to be able to afford a little lavishness. Robin treated everyone who worked with him or for him as an equal, and in return they idolised him.

In the departure lounge he met up with several colleagues who were attending the same conference, one of whom had graduated with him and was now on the staff of Guy's Hospital. They were friendly enough to be able to pull each other's legs, and invariably did so.

'When is the flagship of the Thatcher Revolution going to be torpedoed?' he enquired with a grin.

'Not until all you chaps have jumped off your out-of-date ships!' was the equally apposite reply from the other man.

Robin had little time for the blundering doctrinaire changes being put into operation by the Government. There was a need to streamline the NHS and above all cut down on the vast army of unnecessary second-rate managers, but none of the views of the Government had been tested. This government's arrogance had bankrupted the national wealth by selling the 'family silver' and wasting our oil resources. It was prepared to let money rule every principle it had - or rather, lack of principle. Given a chance, it would sell the national blood transfusion services to a plutocratic vampire, if the money was right. It was a government by a party which was interested only in itself and in making a fast buck wherever it could. This left the NHS underfunded.

'I bet the time will come when Guy's Hospital will become expendable and you'll be sold down the river, or fall victim to a take-over bid' said Robin. 'This is a government of Brutuses. You're all pawns on a political chessboard -- just like the Democratic Union of Mineworkers!'

There was more laughter, as by then they had been joined by their other colleagues. They moved on to the topic of the day; the worrying situation in the Middle East.

Two weeks previously, on 2nd August, Iraq had invaded Kuwait. Iraq's excuse was that Kuwait was stealing oil from Iraq by drilling diagonally into an adjoining border oilfield. Iraq was also not prepared to repay Kuwaiti money which it had borrowed during the Iran-Iraq war. Furthermore, Saddam Hussein had argued that Kuwait was part of Iraq. The rest of the world also knew Saddam had facilities for chemical and biological warfare, and was developing a nuclear armoury.

Several of those discussing this event had either been to the Middle East or had a Middle Eastern clientèle and had a working knowledge of Levantine culture and psychology. It would be too great a loss of face for Saddam Hussein to withdraw from Kuwait; his army of occupation would need to be thrown out.

The American military saw a unique chance of putting to the test its high technology missiles. It was too good an opportunity to miss. There were also oil considerations. To the thinking élite, the Falklands war had been not so much a matter of national pride as a matter of propping up a Prime Minister and a government which was heading, at the time, for electoral unpopularity. It had chosen not to take seriously the reports of the intelligence services, and had been caught off guard.

The lives of young, untrained men had mattered little to a political party which seemed without compassion. If it meant keeping in power a party which was arrogant enough to repeatedly proclaim that a mandate from a minority vote was true democracy, this government would not hesitate to once again sacrifice such young men on the altar of their self-centred canons. That same Prime Minister and her now tired but subservient cabinet were once again in a politically toxic mood, and another military confrontation would suit them well.

They would go along with the USA as its fifty-second state, and widows and orphans would matter little.

These medical leaders could not help feeling that there was likely to be yet another 'local' war. It was simply a matter of when. They were aware that lethal weapons of all sorts in the hands of both sides would bring the London hospitals into the front line, and they doubted whether they were geared to cope with the resulting casualties. Some of them had come across servicemen who had returned from the Falklands both physically and psychologically maimed.

Iraq was doubtless banking on disagreements between the major Western nations, and the position of France was still unclear. As they waited to board their flight, the British group jokingly rounded on the only Frenchman among them.

Didier Delacroix, an agrégé in Paris, was spending a year in Leeds with Bob Hirst as a Research Fellow on a Satra grant. He was known to his French colleagues as Dédé from his initials, but in England his colleagues liked the sound of his first name and he was universally called Didier, which pleased him enormously.

He was an able clinician with a good scientific brain. Many years previously he had worked in England and collected membership of one of the colleges. He spoke English fluently, but whenever he got excited he reverted to his native French. He had a good sense of humour and on this occasion was game to be the butt of his Anglo-Saxon colleagues.

'Maid Marianne is a discriminating girl' he retorted smilingly. 'She is not prepared to bed with John Bull or Uncle Sam until she knows what their hidden intentions are. You see, she prefers a life-long bond to a short affair of convenience. That is the Latin blood in her.'

'Point taken!' replied Robin, laughing.

The General had already been briefed on the expected role of some of the London hospitals in the event of a prolonged clash in the Middle East. It housed the three most vital departments to the treatment of war casualties, those for plastic, thoracic and neurological surgery. Just the same, the other departments would become involved, and Robin felt disquiet about this.

'I would rather the Americans took over all the battle arrangements' said Bob Hirst, who before he had become a consultant in Leeds had been in the Army. 'Their firepower and their high technology could bring it to an end in no time. After all, they taught the Israelis how to wage a modern war, and look how successful they've been. We certainly don't want Israel to become involved, but a war in the Middle East must not be used as a means of keeping a certain lady in power.'

It was well documented that the Israelis had won the seven-day war by the surprise destruction of the Egyptian Air Force and the erroneous intelligence the Egyptians had been fed by the Russians. The Falklands War, having been planned overtly, took no one by surprise, though the second-rate Argentinian Air Force had still managed to inflict appalling casualties on the British Task Force. Furthermore it had been something of a half-hearted war, and the spurious ethics about the sinking of the Belgrano made little sense to the man in the street. If the same attitude was to prevail now, the London hospitals would have to cope with unpleasant casualties.

The mood was certainly critical. As a thinking group, the consensus favoured a cool approach, with a political solution rather than a military one. To the Americans the fear of more than half the world's oil reserves eventually falling into the hands of a ruthless dictator was undoubtedly worrying, and world economy was very relevant. Oil is not just oil - it is politics.

To a professional group on whom the responsibility of coping with horrendous casualties would fall, the humanitarian aspect transcended politics. A political solution seemed preferable, but no one doubted the shrewdness of Saddam Hussein and his determination to have his own way and conduct his own Mein Kampf in the Middle East. Having conquered Kuwait, he would not let go his prey unless driven out of it by military force or world pressure. There was a clear need for a summit conference between the main world powers to evolve the necessary strategy.

The discussion was halted by a call for boarding in numerical order. Robin was in a non-smoking area at 29A, a window seat. The plane was not full and seats B and C were unoccupied. He slipped his jacket off and settled down to study in greater detail the programme of the conference while waiting for the plane to take off.

His peace was soon disturbed by the stewardess as she showed another passenger to seat 29C. Georgiana had made it, just in time. She pushed her holdall into the luggage rack and dropped into her seat with a loud 'phew'.

Robin looked at her. 'That was a close shave' he said with a welcoming smile.

'I got delayed on the motorway. The idiots flashed a slow-down signal just past a slip road. Why it couldn't have been done earlier I do not understand.'

'You can't expect a ministry run by left-over imbeciles to think intelligently' came the unexpected reply.

Georgiana wondered for a moment about such a remark from a complete stranger. 'In the mood I'm in I'm inclined to agree with you' she said. 'I like being early to get a window seat in a non-smoking area.'

'Please have mine. I didn't ask for one.'

Georgiana hesitated. She had not meant to drop a hint.

'Oh no please, it doesn't matter' she said.

'I insist' said Robin as he got up. He moved out into the aisle and they swapped seats.

Studying her face, he decided that it reflected intelligence. She had wide pale blue-green eyes dotted with soft brown specks; their colour matched her green suit. She had a slightly pale, lemony complexion, and beneath high cheekbones was a face with chiselled features made softer by light auburn hair combed back and held in a well-plaited bun, chignon-style. Her make-up had been sparingly applied. Her face, he reflected, did not need it. It displayed beauty and more than a suggestion of sensuality. He felt a natural and instant attraction to her.

He had an odd feeling that he had seen this woman before. He turned towards her and leaned across the empty seat.

'Since we are going to be neighbours for the next five hours, may I introduce myself. Robin, Robin Chesham. I have a feeling I've met you before.'

Her eyes lit up. 'THE Robin Chesham?'

Robin was too experienced to be caught out by flattery. 'I'm the Robin Chesham who's going to the Satra meeting' he responded.

'Snap!' she said. 'Georgiana Gilmour. I noticed you were chairing the first afternoon session. I'm going to be speaking just before you in the morning session.'

'I thought Ken Taylor was giving that talk?'

'He was, but he has to attend a selection committee for the appointment of a new cardiologist tomorrow evening. I've had to take his place.'

'How strange' said Robin. 'I'm going for precisely the opposite reason. I want to avoid sitting on a Senior Registrar Selection Committee. It'll be a stitched-up appointment and I didn't want to be part of it.'

'I thought that sort of thing could never happen?' she said, rather naively.

'There are ways and means, unfortunately. And there is still patronage in our profession. We have a research registrar doing some flawed work on flow cytometry for the professor, and when I pointed this out the work was already advanced, so my views were disregarded. He will nevertheless be rewarded with an MD for his thesis. And for his servility. But it will hardly be worth the paper it's written on.'

'But will the assessors pass it?'

'I was going to be one of them, but for various reasons, not any more.'

'What about the other short-listed candidates?'

'You can manipulate the field you want. The shortlist is left with the professor and the chairman of the selection committee. The chairman just happens to be a poodle of the academic head. So you can see why I don't want to be part of the appointment. The system works on reaching universal agreement, and if you're there you are deemed to have gone along with it. I wasn't prepared to do so.'

'I'm amazed' said Georgiana. 'I hope this sort of thing doesn't happen often.'

'Fortunately not - but it can. Anyway, I shall be only too glad to have a day to myself in Helsinki tomorrow. Wednesday is my free day anyway, so I don't feel guilty about it. I want to visit the Sibelius Monument again. Have you been to Helsinki before?'

'No' she replied. 'I'm just looking forward to strolling around, perhaps to-morrow. Will you be staying at The Europa? That's where

I'll be.'

'Yes, I think all the speakers are staying there. It's convenient, and there are good conference facilities. It's not far from one of the main streets, the Boulevardi. There are some good restaurants there, serving the Opera House. It's quite central and close to the bus routes.'

'Sounds ideal.'

'Not bad. Helsinki is not such a big city and it's easy to visit. Right now it's in the middle of the celebrations for the University's 350th anniversary. They had the international do last week, and the national one is early next month.'

'You obviously know the place well.'

'Not that well, but Satra has hosted me there before, when the project was being developed, so I had the chance to get to know the more interesting sites. The Finns are very proud of Sibelius. The monument is very moving. Do you like his music?'

'Can't say I'm terribly familiar with it, but I do know Finlandia.'

Robin's eyes lit up. 'It gives you a great insight into his love of his country – all those pine and birch forests and the lakes' he said. 'If you'd like to see the monument, I'd be delighted to take you there. There's a bus – No 18, I think. It gets you there in no time. Or we could walk. It's only a mile or so, and there's plenty to see on the way.'

'How very nice of you. I'd like to take you up on that.'

'Great! We could go there mid-morning, enjoy a walk by the sea or along the Tooloo Lake and then have lunch near the monument on the way back.'

'You obviously enjoy Sibelius?' she said, wanting to keep the conversation going.

'I like a lot of good music. Sibelius is a post-romantic who has moved away from the imaginative approach of the great composers of last century.'

'What's your kind of music?'

'I suppose it's a mishmash of classical and modern, including dance music. I must be a romantic at heart. All evocative music appeals to me.'

'I was playing Bruch's Violin Concerto by Tasmin Little on the way to London. Do you like Bruch?'

'How interesting. It's a favourite of mine. I find the second movement one of the most moving pieces of music I know. It makes me dream.' He turned to her. 'But how amazing that you too like Little's interpretation. I saw it advertised in a music magazine recently and ordered it. She's delightful to watch. Have you noticed how she seems to be making eyes at the conductor all the time?'

'Perhaps the conductor started it!' said Georgiana, with a mischievous smile.

'That's always possible.' he smiled back. 'What's interesting about this recording is that it's by the Royal Liverpool Philharmonic Orchestra. You probably know that Bruch was Director there before Hallé took over. By then he had already composed his Violin Concerto. Little's interpretation is very stirring and sensitive. It really brings out the tenderness of the second movement.'

There was a short pause in the conversation as Robin looked round to see where the drinks trolley was. Then he turned back to Georgiana.

'I'm curious about the appointment of a cardiologist. Is there a heavy demand locally?'

'This is a second post. We have an ageing population of retired people in the area and the demand is increasing.'

'Where do you send your cases for surgery?'

'Usually to Southampton, I believe. For two reasons. One is that we're part of the Wessex Region; the other is that we think the Southampton results are better than the Bristol ones, though patients do have to travel further.'

'When Bath broke away from Bristol in the late sixties to join the

Wessex Region, didn't they feel the Bristol mafia were keeping certain advantages for themselves? I think Bath had a good all-round team and felt a little cheated.'

Robin paused before replying, as if to choose his words carefully.

'I heard about the outcome of some of Bristol's interventions. I gather there is some discomfort about certain results not being as good as those elsewhere. I also remember some two years ago a damning television programme about the unit, as well as some rumblings about results in children.'

'Yes, there was' replied Georgiana. 'The rumour in Bath, true or false, was that the follow-up reports on patients referred from the South-West were not quite what would be expected.'

* * * * * * * * *

Back at the General, the selection committee had met and the four short-listed candidates had been interviewed. An hour-long discussion had then followed, as no agreement could be reached. The regional assessor felt that no appointment should be made, as the calibre of the candidates was below the standard he had expected and he could not believe that better candidates had not applied. His contention was that the post should be re-advertised, which had displeased the chairman.

The non-surgical hospital committee member was of the opinion that the local candidate did not have the stature for such a post, but this was contested by the Professor of Surgery. A consensus opinion could not be reached, and the disagreement was such that the chairman suggested the committee should take a break and re-assemble fifteen minutes later. The secretary was sent to tell the candidates that they need not wait and that the decision of the committee would be conveyed to them in writing. They knew what this meant. The most disturbed was the local candidate.

When the committee reassembled it was clear that no member

was prepared to change his standpoint, and that therefore no appointment could be made. After everyone had left, the chairman and the professor stayed behind to talk.

They had a problem on their hands. They sensed the turmoil that would follow, and strangely enough were glad that Robin Chesham had not been there, as they thought his strong views would have made matters worse. It did not cross their minds for a moment that it was their lack of judgment and their machinations that had led to his decision to drop out. They were so engrossed in their own petty political power that they had failed to see the dangers inherent in a system too intent on patronage and insider manipulations.

Dark clouds were slowly gathering for them.

* * * * * * * *

The drinks trolley had reached row 29, and the steward was offering a range of apéritifs.

'How would you like a glass of bubbly?' Robin asked Georgiana.

'That sounds good.'

'Then be my guest. Can we have a bottle of your dry Moêt et Chandon?'

Robin knew this was the only champagne on board, so there was no showing off about it. The steward obliged and they settled down to a chat over the wine and their meal.

Robin was interested in his travelling companion's background. He wanted to know where she had taken her honours degree, where she had worked previously and how she saw her future. The more he listened to her, the more his attraction for her grew, though he was careful not to show it. She in turn asked about his work, though she was already aware of his various contributions to his discipline.

'You have the reputation of being as much a physician as a surgeon' she said. 'What made you lean towards surgery?'

'Possibly two reasons. One - and it goes back a long way - I took a BSc Physiology as an intercalated honours degree and since then I have kept a certain passion for correcting malfunction with drugs rather than with a knife. Also it allowed me to earn a few bucks by helping foreign students get through their physiology exams, while realising how important the subject is. The second reason is that I simply love using my hands.'

Again he paused for a few seconds to consider his words.

'I enjoy the sensuality of my hands. What they tell me, what they can do, what they can communicate to others. I suppose all technicians feel that way.'

'Some more than others' she commented.

They continued to chat over the meal, and at Robin's invitation followed it with a liqueur. By the time the plane landed just before eleven, they were both in a congenial mood.

In the airport building on the way to the immigration desks, Robin introduced Georgiana to his other colleagues. Didier kissed her hand in his Gallic way and monopolised her in the slow-moving queue. Satra had provided a courtesy coach to take them all to the hotel, and Georgiana sat with Robin once again.

It was past midnight when they reached the hotel and booked in. The speakers were all on the same floor. Georgiana and Robin found themselves in rooms opposite each other, with Robin's at the front, facing east with a view across the harbour and the peninsula beyond.

'I'll call you to organise the morning if I don't see you at breakfast' Robin said.

'I shall look forward to that' was the reply.

'It will be my pleasure.'

Georgiana unpacked her case and hung up her garments. The room was unduly warm. The bedcover had already been pulled back, and after her long day the soft sheets beckoned. She undressed completely, took her vanity bag to the bathroom and attended to her face and teeth, feeling too tired for a bath. Her mind roamed over the events of the day: the long chat on the plane, covering so many subjects; the champagne; Robin's easy and unpresumptuous manners; the invitation for the next day; the anticipation of the conference. She slumped naked over the bed and mused for a while about her day's experience.

'An attractive man' she murmured to herself, wondering idly about the unfamiliar emotions she was feeling. But when she tucked herself under the bedsheet and turned the light off, she was unconscious in no time.

* * * * * * * *

Robin's room across the corridor was a well-appointed one; conference chairmen are richly pampered. A king-size bed occupied half the wall on one side. A wide french window opened on to a balcony overlooking the well-lit waterfront. In the corner opposite the bed was a small bar with wine glasses and flutes, with a fridge underneath. He opened it and stuck his bottle of champagne inside.

Over the bar, in the angle of the walls, a concealed light cast a warm glow on to the ceiling above. It had come on automatically on Robin's entry, but could be equally well switched on or off from the bedside. Two comfortable armchairs and a sizeable desk with a matching chair hardly intruded in that large room. It had all the cosiness of a bridal junior suite.

A frosted glass door in the corner opposite the bar opened into the bathroom, with a commodious corner bath and a double-bowl washing unit provided with guest combs, toothbrushes and toothpaste. A heated towel rail filled the gap between a bidet and the toilet pan. On two pegs next to the towel rail hung two cream towelling bathrobes. There was about it all an impression of overindulgence, but that hardly concerned Robin. He was still wondering where he had seen Georgiana before. He knew her face, the high cheek bones, the wide blue-green eyes, even the manner in which she spoke. There was a strange feeling of déja vu about her.

He lay back, closed his eyes and, still in his undressed state, yielded insensibly to the night.

CHAPTER THREE

Georgiana rose early as usual, but she began her morning quietly and did not go downstairs to breakfast until just before nine. Spotting some of the other delegates, including Didier, there, she joined them for a leisurely meal.

Robin, meanwhile, had decided on a grasse matinée and skipped his breakfast. Instead, he had chosen to soak himself in his enormous bath with a good book for the best part of an hour. It was a favourite recreation of his, one he would normally indulge in after a day's work and before his evening meal. It was his way of relaxing, and he had missed it the night before.

At home, his wife would often run his bath for him in their en suite while he checked up on his calls. He would then collect his morning mail and take it upstairs to be read in the bath while unwinding. Either before or after having his bath, he would often make love to his wife, a pleasure which could be extended if their two children were not home from university. Time spent enjoying each other physically was always a bonding occasion for them.

At ten o'clock Robin decided it was time to fulfil his promise of the previous evening. He knocked on the door of Georgiana's room.

She had been awaiting impatiently for him and was ready. She was wearing a pale aquamarine loose cotton T-shirt with appliqué and embroidery on the front, in the same green as her trousers, the same ones she had travelled in the day before.

She was now wearing her hair down. Robin noticed the difference it made to her face, but thought it had been more attractive with her hair combed away. Perhaps the nakedness of her neck made her look more voluptuous.

As they took the lift to go downstairs they decided to walk rather than take a bus. In the foyer, Robin unfolded a small map of the city and went over the route. Georgiana was happy to be guided by him.

It was a sunny day. The morning mist had lifted from the sea but had still not cleared from the air above, so that the sky was a hazy blue. Robin's casual open neck short-sleeved white shirt, cream trousers and sandals seemed well in keeping with the holiday mood they were in.

'We'll turn left at the next street and go up a couple of blocks to Union Street, as I like to call it' he said. 'It's a long road running south-north and it takes us to Senate Square. There are some of the finest classical buildings in Helsinki up there, dating back to early last century. They were designed by an architect called Carl Ludwig Engel, one of their greatest. The older buildings of the university are up there as well.'

A gentle breeze blew through the crossroads as they made their way to the square where Helsinki Cathedral stands, built in the form of a square cross with pedimented façades on three sides, supported by round Corinthian columns. Their chapters reproduce themselves not only in the pilasters of the adjoining walls but in those of the Empire-style university library on the western side of the square.

'I was here for a university commemoration day once' said Robin. 'It was quite a sight to see all the bigwigs in their special fluted top hats and tails. I'll take you inside the library. You should see the ceiling.'

They walked through to the central part of the library, where more Corinthian pillars supported a splendid circular ceiling. The morning sun was streaming through the windows. Then they retraced their steps back to the square. Georgiana was impressed by the grandeur of the two classical buildings and could see why her companion was so enamoured of the architecture of old Helsinki.

About half a mile west of the square, they reached the railway station on the city's main road, which had been named after its hero and most important military figure, Marshall Carl Mannerheim, who had won Finland back from Russia in 1917. Beyond the station the road borders the 'inland sea' of Toolonlahti Lake, on the southern corner of which stands Finlandia Hall. It is clad in Carrara marble and, in parts, in contrasting local black granite and is a modern architectural delight housing a theatre and conference rooms. From it one could see along the same sea front to its north the new opera house which was under construction. The sight reminded Robin that the opera season had started.

'I noticed in the What's On guide in my room that there are two operas on at the moment' he said. 'One of them's called Vincent – it's apparently about Van Gogh, though I have never heard of it, I'm afraid to say. The other is Verdi's Masked Ball.'

'I don't know that one' she replied. 'My knowledge of Verdi's operas is limited to La Traviata and Rigoletto and some highlights of Aida.'

'Un Ballo in Masquera is of great interest to the Finns because it's based on Gustav the Third of Sweden, the last king to reign over them' explained Robin. 'It is about his assassination at a masked ball, but for political reasons the action was shifted to Boston with an English Earl as the governor of the district. There are some lovely duets in it. Would you be interested to see it? I could try to get tickets for Saturday night, as I suppose will be our only free evening.'

"That would be a great idea."

They stopped for a moment to watch the men at work on the building of the Opera House before turning off the Mannerheimintie into a road bearing the name of Sibelius. This led them to Sibelius Park, an arena of granite broken up by irregular stretches of lawn, at the north side of which stands the Sibelius Monument. Nearer to them a bust of the composer gave the impression of having just sprung out of the rock.

A few pine trees and cypresses added their darker green to the monument's backdrop, which was made up primarily of birch trees whose white bark competed with the pallid metallic splendour of organ-like pipes welded into an imaginative sculpture.

To the west, through a glade of trees separating the park from the coast road, the sun, already passed its meridian, had turned the waters of the bay into a silvery expanse which added still more light to the monument.

They stood in silence to admire the work of Eila Hiltunen, the controversial sculptress of the monument, who had been forced to add to its setting the bust of the composer. A melodic north-west wind blew intermittently through the trees on all sides.

'The music of the wind, the very inspiration of Sibelius' work' said Robin. A fresh gust came down at that moment, blowing lilting, doleful notes through the trees. 'You can hear his Valse Triste.' His voice was full of emotion. Georgiana was moved.

'The whole of Sibelius' music is a series of symphonic poems. You can hear what Shelley felt when he wrote of the West Wind - 'Make me thy lyre even as the forest is'.'

Georgiana stood motionless a foot in front of and to the right of Robin, whose eyes were now firmly fixed on her. She sensed his gaze, and sensed also the depth of the emotions behind his words. She listened to the wind through the trees but was as well hearing the soft echoes of his mellow voice. She turned towards him, her large eyes waking up from a momentary dream.

'It's wonderful. You've given me a new appreciation of Sibelius' work. It's so moving. I'll treasure this moment.'

They walked to the monument and looked at it from below: a

fusion of pan-pipes on which the wind was playing its own tunes. She found it breathtaking.

Robin suggested they cross the coast road on to the edge of the bay, beyond which the land curved back towards a small peninsula. The raggedness of that granite shoreline, with its adjoining woodlands, was a picturesque scenery of dark grey and green reflected into the sea against a background of a pure pale blue sky. They were both conscious of the romance of this moment, but were not prepared to display it to each other; after all, they were still little more than strangers.

'So tranquil' remarked Georgiana. 'This is more like a lake than the sea. There's something nostalgic about lakes. They have a sort of languid noiselessness. They seem to bring out your inner self, but they also evoke nature so powerfully. You feel you're sharing the same air. I remember feeling the same way when I saw Lake Geneva for the first time. I was in Ferney, Voltaire's village.'

'You're quite right, it's so… contemplative. Don't artists just love water! Have you seen that beautiful pre-Raphaelite painting by Waterhouse of the Lady of Shalott, in the Tate? Byron said the lake was 'the mirror where stars and mountains view the stillness of their aspect' and of course he was talking about the same lake. That languor also inspired Lamartine's Le Lac. He also wrote a poem called Jocelyn, where he took up Shelley's and Sibelius' communion with nature and what you're experiencing now. Do you know Lamartine? I can give you this one, if you'll excuse my French.' He began to recite from somewhere deep in his memory.

'Arbres harmonieux, sapins! harpe des bois,
Où tous les vents du ciel modulent une voix,
Vous êtes l'instrument où tout pleure, où tout chante,
Où de ses mille échos la nature s'enchante,
Où, dans les deux accents d'un souffle aérien,
Tout homme a le soupir d'accord avec le sien.'

Moved as she was, Georgiana was beginning to feel it was time to come back to earth.

'You fibber! I have been told your French is fluent, so let's have less of this false modesty.'

'Who told you that?'

'Didier. He said that in a guest lecture you gave in France your French was superb. And you spoke without notes.'

'I shall have to speak to him about that' beamed Robin.

This little interlude brought them back to earth a little. It was time to start walking back past the monument again, as Robin had booked a table for lunch.

'We'll follow the coast road back' he said. 'I took the liberty of booking lunch at an interesting restaurant called the Elite for around one o'clock. I hope you'll approve.'

'I'm being very spoilt.'

'Why not? In fact I am the one being spoilt. If you hadn't been here I wouldn't have had anyone to show the sights of the Daughter of the Baltic to. It is so difficult when you're at a conference to take time off just to enjoy a place. It's been nice sharing this break with you.'

'You don't have to use my whole first name, you know. It's a bit of a mouthful. I usually get called Georgie, sometimes Gina. Sometimes it's even Gigi, but I'd rather you didn't call me that. Your choice.'

'Well, I have carte blanche then. In which case I shall give you a name of my own choosing. I shall simply call you G.'

She smiled, eyes full of approbation. No one had called her by that before.

As they walked down to the end of the coastal road, Robin explained how the Elite was the haunt of artists, writers, actors, musicians and similar patrons and was known for its special coffee. They turned into Hesperian-katu and were soon in the restaurant. It was a quaint place with pictures of the famous on its walls as if they were trophies.

They now felt very much at ease with each other and their conversation began to roam more freely. They were almost vying with each other to sculpt their words. After a cup of the Elite's famous Flaming Tango coffee, they made their way back past the National Museum and the Parliament. They stopped off so that Robin could show Georgiana where the Sibelius Academy was. It was nearly four o'clock when they reached the Europa.

'What time is the reception?' enquired Robin at the desk.

'Seven for registration, followed by drinks at half past and dinner afterwards' was the reply.

They parted company, arranging to meet again at seven at the welcoming reception.

* * * * * * * *

When Robin got to his room he found a note from the chairman of the first session, Gustav Borg, asking for a meeting with him at five to organise the first day to make sure there would be no overlap in the content of the lectures. He recognised a good chairman would always see to such matters. They had a long and friendly chat. Gustav wanted to know more about the changes taking place in the UK in the NHS, which he thought was being senselessly politicised. They were both, however, looking forward to the evening.

The reception and dinner took place in a jovial atmosphere. Robin had suggested that Georgiana join him and Didier at one of the tables. It was a casual evening - a meeting of old friends - and Didier was canvassing for attendees to his bi-annual Journées régionales hépato-gastroentérologiques in the coming November. He would book his speakers into the Concorde-Lafayette Hotel, as this was closest to his hospital in Paris.

'Robin, I want you to be one of my speakers. Will you come please?' asked Didier. Robin pulled out his diary. He valued Didier's friendship and was happy to help.

'What are the dates?' he enquired as he leafed through the pages for November.

'Tuesday the 20th to Saturday 24th.'

'I can move some of my commitments, but you'd better let me know more fully what you're planning.'

Didier looked very pleased. 'Très bien, mon ami' he said, leaving them to recruit other speakers.

Soon after that, the evening broke up. Robin thanked Georgiana for being such an attentive and willing companion and bade her goodnight. To her, the night seemed to have barely begun. She wished they could have spent more of it together.

CHAPTER FOUR

In the undisturbed stillness of his room, Robin thought about the exultant emotions that had been troubling him all day. In his restive state of mind, he found himself drifting into a reverie of his youth. He was naturally self-analytical and good at retracing events that had triggered off his feelings or his views, but on this occasion he felt vacuous. His mind roamed back to the first time he had fallen properly in love.

It had been the second Saturday of the Michaelmas term, the term following his graduation, and Robin had gone with his flatmate to a Saturday University Union hop, following one of those spontaneous impulses so often used as a lazy way of killing time. Robin and his flatmate now held junior appointments at their Medical School Hospital. As students they had shared a two-bedroom flat off Russell Square. They had decided to keep it during these appointments for social convenience. It was a stone's throw from the Union dance hall.

Robin's generation had pioneered what was to become the permissive society of the sixties. when the advent of the Pill had suddenly liberated women from the fear of pregnancy and showed their sexuality to be no different from men's. It was the avant garde of an adapted version of the proto-Bloomsbury philosophy.

It had been an age of intense individualism, with every bygone creed questioned. Robin had joined the university's Rationalist Society and had belonged to a vocal core which had treated itself to numerous relationships, serial as well as parallel. They had not been solely for lust. They were all experiments in loving liaisons: affection and tenderness had always framed them. Partings were never quarrels, and former lovers remained long-term friends.

Now that he was at the threshold of professional life and rich in emotional experience, had responsibility and clinical accountability changed the questioning philosophy of his student days? From a roving attachment to self-indulgence and adventure, was he now subconsciously sensing an awareness of compelling stability?

In the dance hall, by a twist of chance, he had met an ex-girlfriend of his, Alison, who had talked a non-dancing friend of hers into coming to the hop for a break.

'Meet Sam, my closest friend' Alison said. 'We're in the same hall of residence.' He found himself being introduced to a tastefully-dressed, mesomorphic young woman, whose deep blue eyes radiated an unconcealed intelligence and whose mellifluous voice seemed to hide a certain element of sorrow. He felt intensely attracted to her.

'What are you studying?' he enquired, to start a conversation.

'I'm in my final year of an Honours Degree in Psychology. I took Physiology as my subsidiary, but it's finished now.'

'Is it hard?'

'Yes. The final year schedule is a heavy one and I'm already feeling the strain.'

'Well, it was sensible of you to take a break tonight.'

'I'm not a dancer, but Alison was very persuasive.'

'Never mind. Let's take the floor. It'll do you good.'

Robin was an inveterate dancer. He offered his hand and gently led her to the floor.

'You have a bruise on your wrist' she said.

'Just a minor injury. We played football against the Charing Cross team this afternoon and one of the players accidentally trod on my hand.'

'You play a lot?'

'A fair bit.'

Indeed, Robin was a hardened player who took to the pitch every possible Saturday. He was in both the medical school and the university team. He was a talented striker, agile and swift, who usually played centre-forward. He was also a boxer.

In spite of her protestations about being a non-dancer, Sam followed him closely, her long, light ash-blonde hair flowing freely as they moved. A fleshy, musky perfume emanated from her body. His attraction to her intensified and he felt drawn by emotions that were new to him.

After their first dance, they rejoined Alison and Robin offered them both a drink. While he was at the bar, Sam quizzed Alison about him, still taking him to be a student.

'I gather he was one of the brightest in his year' said Alison. 'But he is also a bit of a lad. He's pretty hot in the sack as well. You'll like him.'

They were laughing at the remark as Robin was coming back with the drinks. Robin monopolised Sam for the rest of the evening, by which time he had become deeply attached to her.

As they took to the floor for the last time, he invited her to his flat. She was somewhat hesitant about it.

'I'll walk you back to the Hall afterwards' he reassured her.

'OK' she said, with a cautious smile. It was not until Sam was in his flat that she realised that Robin was already qualified and in a job.

They talked without constraint. She shared with him a keen interest in art, poetry and music, having been taught the piano at public school. He too enjoyed playing the piano, but she did not share his interest in sport.

They talked late into the night, about each other, their studies, their work, their philosophy of life and their aspirations. They were both ambitious individuals.

Sam felt a strong affinity for Robin, but past experiences made her reluctant to acknowledge or show such feelings. Robin had no such reservations; he could not take his eyes off her. He was feeling something he had not felt before and was beginning to realise that he had suddenly, unexpectedly, fallen in love. He had an intense wish to make love to Sam, but it was part of his nature never to rush. He always wanted the desire to be mutual. This was part of his hedonistic belief that pleasure should be synchronized, but it also derived from a genuine respect for the female gender. Seduction had to be enjoyed as a two-way traffic in which both bodies were to be equally and simultaneously pleasured.

It was well past midnight when Robin walked Sam back to the Hall. They shared a brief parting kiss. They agreed to meet again the next afternoon. Perhaps they could spend an hour or so at the Wallace Collection, which she had not yet visited.

Alison saw Sam at breakfast.

'Did you have a nice evening?' she asked, with a little mocking smile.

Sam replied in the affirmative.

'He's good fun, isn't he?' said Alison. Before Sam could answer her, she said, almost maliciously: 'Did he make love to you?'

'As a matter of fact, no. He didn't try to get physical at all. He couldn't have been more of a gentleman.'

'That's him all over. I had to wait till the fourth date before he finally got round to giving me what I wanted! But once he made a move, he became irresistible. We were friends for quite a while. He was a wonderful person to be with. Always attentive, always fun. He made you feel loved, all the time.'

Sam too had found his company exhilarating. He had shown so much interest in how she thought and felt, and what she would do when she graduated. No one before had shown so much interest in her.

Alison listened to her attentively and realised that she could easily become besotted with Robin. Sam being her closest friend, she felt she could be open.

'Don't get jealous if you see him with other girls' she said. 'He tends to have several girlfriends on the go at once. He is very honest about his relationships. The trouble is, he's so nice and so lovable that it's difficult to fall out with him. And no one makes love like him. It's never the same twice. You never get bored. He's an addiction. He spoils you for other men.'

'I'm seeing him again this afternoon.'

'Well, you won't find a more engaging person. He took to you very quickly last night. You must have sparked off something deep for him to have shown so much interest so quickly. You're lucky.'

After their visit to the Wallace Collection, Robin had invited Sam to stay for supper, which he cooked. They enjoyed it with a full-blooded red burgundy, wine being a further interest of Robin.

'Where does your name come from?' he asked as they ate.

'I got it at Roedean. It's from my initials. My first name is Sonia from my mother's second name, she's Swedish. My father wanted Anthea for my second name and my surname is Maynard.'

'You may be Sam to the rest of the world. To me now, I want you to be my Anthea.'

Sam was taken aback by such a whim. Was he giving her a different personality - was he imprinting his own more powerful one on hers? It worried her a little, but, like it or not, she would forever now be his Anthea.

This was the first of many evenings they were to spend together. Robin gave her all the dates when he would be off duty in the evening and said he would want to see her and no one else on those days. When she heard this, Alison told Sam he must have fallen in love with her. This was not usual for him. Yet, apart from warm parting kisses, Robin had made no attempt to seduce her. Did he feel she was not ready to accept him? None the less, when on duty he rang her every evening. When off duty he had to be with her. The world outside hardly mattered any more.

Yet he and Anthea were spheres apart. She was the only child of affluent parents from Carlisle, overprotected, self-centred, nurtured in the cosiness of Roedean, elegantly dressed but matter-of-fact in her philosophy of life, perhaps even unyielding. For a twenty-one-year-old, there was still something coltish about her. The strong element of music and art in her boarding school had left their imprint on her, and this interest she shared with him. She had taken him to visit her school perched on the Sussex Downs overlooking the sea, insulated by fifty acres of land from the rest of the world and rich in sports facilities which interested her not at all.

Robin was a product of state schooling, of the big new comprehensives, the last but one of five children of a not-so-moneyed family, used to sharing and understanding, yet sensitive, cautious and unpretentious. Above all, he loved pleasure seeking and was a practising romantic, something he had inherited from the cultural impact of a half-French mother. He had enjoyed his student days to the full and had more experience of life and of the opposite sex than most of his contemporaries.

As he got to love her more and more, he also understood how ill-prepared she was for university life, which had taken her by surprise. She was sexually naive and constantly felt threatened by young males on the prowl. He had sensed in her that apprehensiveness and was aware of her defensive attitude to his physical assertiveness.

For a student of psychology such fears seem hard to fathom, but as she came to realise his deep love for her she relaxed more and more and was able to open her heart to him. Natural curiosity rather than carnal desire had led, during her first collegiate year, to her only two physical experiences of men, and both had been disastrous. They had both followed evenings of pub crawling. On the first occasion, in her very first term, following the rag on Guy Fawkes night, she had ended up in Regent's Park. It was a cold night, the grass was wet and it was all over in a matter of minutes. Was this what it was all about? No protective had been used, and for weeks afterwards she had lived in fear of pregnancy and of what her parents would say. To make matters worse, there had been no sequel to that seemingly shallow and impulsive occasion. She had felt cheated and used.

The following spring, hesitant yet curious, eager not to remain a neophyte, she had allowed herself to undergo a similar hapless experience, one that had led her to believe that such executions were always ephemeral and purely for the gratification of the male. Exchanges of confidences with other female students simply reinforced these fears. It all left her disconsolate, even withdrawn. Her apparent vivaciousness was just a cover veiling from the world the sorrow of these two experiences.

Robin felt still greater tenderness for her, and told her what a beautiful and bonding act sex can be when done with affection, understanding and love. Perhaps as a student of pure psychology she was too versed in a world of theory and pseudoscience, a world alien to the blunt realities of life. Yet she knew her mind well enough to know what she could come to terms with, and live with.

In an effort to give solace to her sorrow, he pointed out to her that her past unfortunate exposures to the opportunist male needed to be treated as minor accidents that were common to many of her contemporaries in the real world. Their memory would become entombed under the sands of time and eventually refreshed by re-experimentation. He spent hours assuaging her fears. Though she often willingly stayed nights or whole weekends with him, he held back from invading her body. She enjoyed the naked warmth of his body and the comfort of close proximity to him, without the wish for total belonging.

In late November of that year, as the term was coming to an end, he had talked her, in spite of her aversion to dancing, to attending with him the hospital end-of-the-year ball. He wanted her to meet his many friends. He wanted them to see his happiness.

As it happened, the evening turned out to be one of the most enjoyable he ever had. She had looked radiant, and had felt elated to see him so blissfully happy. She had come back afterwards to his flat and stayed the night. Then as an unhurried autumn dawn broke and woke them up, while wrapped in his embrace and aroused by his caresses, she had felt the urge to be possessed, and finally offered herself to him.

She was surprised by the amorousness of his hands and the gentleness of his movements, yet was aware of the strength of his passion and astounded by the time he took to allow her to savour every new sensation that was now flooding through her. It seemed to have blotted from her mind, at least for the moment, her two previous misfortunes, and with her consequent fervid willingness he found himself more and more bonded to her.

'I feel like Christina Rosetti when she wrote her poem A Birthday' he told her. She was not sure she knew it. He offered to recite the first stanza of the poem:

My heart is like a singing bird
Whose nest is in a watered shoot:
My heart is like an apple-tree
Whose boughs are bent with thickest fruit:
My heart is like a rainbow shell

That paddles in a halcyon sea;
My heart is gladder than all these
Because my love is come to me.

Alison had been right. He had fallen in love with her.

When Anthea left for the Christmas break, he lived in longing for her and could hardly await her return in January. He had written to her every day and the intensity of his feelings and his overt romanticism overwhelmed her, almost frightened her.

Months of utter rapture had passed without heartache, though Anthea occasionally voiced her inability to be always on his wavelength emotionally or physically. June was approaching, and her finals were looming. She was showing some degree of anxiety. As a break he had taken her to Ascot on the Thursday, Lady's Day. She had enjoyed that experience, and she had looked gorgeous in a chiffon dress and big pink hat.

If her experiences of the male had by now been apparently repatterned, inside she was still suffering from their imprint on her ego. She found Robin's amorous activities too torrid and exhausting. He would often make love to her several times a day if the opportunity arose. He never rushed it, and the utilitarian in her had once even timed it to last a full thirty-five minutes.

He had suggested that she should find a job in London on graduating and live with him with a lifelong relationship in mind, but she feared the displeasure of her rather old-fashioned parents at the idea. At least, that was her excuse.

On the several occasions when he went to Oxford for soccer matches, he took her with him, but she really went to please him. It was usual for the coach to detour to Sonning and stop at The Swan for refreshments. They would then go for a short, loving walk along the river to enjoy the tranquillity there. He loved the reflection of her face and her flowing flaxen hair in the peaceful waters of the Thames. He could not dream of a future without her. But in her down-to-earth way she had decided that his physical side, be it his sexual athleticism or his sub-aggressive enjoyment of sports, including boxing, as well as his passion for dancing, was too much for her to cope with. She feared the results of a union which produced scions.

Accordingly, after obtaining a degree with distinction in her two main subjects, she had written to him from Carlisle saying that she did not think she could sustain their present intense relationship and had decided to accept a post in Leeds.

Robin was devastated. The summer months left him agonising over their relationship and pining for her. He blamed himself for being so demanding and so physically active, but in spite of an ardent correspondence with her he failed to keep the lines open. She had been his dream girl, whose happiness was to be his life's fulfilment. She had given him a purpose, an aim, a wish to be a hospital specialist: a life of plenty in a home of comfort. How could he unlove what he loved? He could not hate her instead. How does one unlearn a poem one has memorised? How does one un-memorise a memory?

The void she had left was immense. He made contact again with several past girlfriends, all too keen to be with him again; relating to women had never been a problem for him. But no one could fill the emptiness left by Anthea. The emotional energy released by her absence had to be directed elsewhere, and he found solace by directing his full fires to his work. From consultancy having been just an aim, he abruptly had a burning ambition to be among the best. His love for Anthea was being translated into a passion for medical research, and he was unlikely ever to waver from it.

It had been a traumatic experience and now, somehow, he was

again feeling the very emotions that had once triggered his love for Anthea. It perturbed him, because two years after Anthea had left and he had made an enormous effort to suppress and overcome it all, he had reinvested his emotions in a wife he adored and who shared his hedonistic views on life and enjoyed his ever-permutating lovemaking. The years had strengthened their bond and he thought nothing would change it. Everything about Anthea had long been buried, cocooned deep in his subconscious and concreted away from his memory. Yet in his reverie, the fervency of the emotions that had sparked off that sudden and ground-breaking relationship of more than twenty-five years previously had sprung again. He was not remembering Anthea, whose features had long been blotted out of his consciousness; he was simply revisiting a dormant emotion, and since the experience left him disturbed and baffled, he had to convince himself of the need for an inner equipoise to come to terms with what was now bewitching him.

He broke his reverie, got up from his armchair and decided it was time to organise himself for the next day and go to bed.

CHAPTER FIVE

Gustav Borg was the conference organiser. He was also a dependable chairman. As such, he made sure he was the first down to breakfast on the Thursday morning to give himself time to check on the facilities required by the speakers. The previous evening he had done the round of them all and agreed on the contents of their talks after his meeting with Robin, to avoid any embarrassing duplication of subject matter.

He was joined at his breakfast table by Carl Rieger, who had come from Vienna, and Lars Nordin from Norway. A few minutes later Georgiana arrived, and all three men, with immaculate politeness, stood to greet her to their table.

She was wearing a houndstooth check skirt in oatmeal and black and a matching oatmeal blouse carrying a wide bow at the front. Its long puffed sleeves showed just beyond those of her simple but elegant pure wool short jacket in red, trimmed with black braid, to match the black of her skirt. It looked comfortable and appeared the ideal attire to lecture in.

Robin arrived shortly afterwards, and the professional style of the dress was not lost on him. He had always admired well-turned-out women.

The lecture room was well equipped and had excellent acoustics. Satra must have been pleased with the attendance of over ninety guests on top of the local specialists.

The medical profession, once known for its good manners had over the previous decade lost its courtesy towards the drug houses.

Many were the doctors who would exploit them for sponsorship to meetings but fail to attend them. Worst of all, invitations to dinners, though accepted, were all too frequently not honoured. Yet pharmaceutical companies got a bad press, and much of it stemmed from the way the profession behaved. All the hospitality has to be paid for, and eventually it is reflected in the price of drugs.

On the other hand, letters to sales managers or medical directors are all too often not answered. These companies are therefore not always blameless. On this occasion, however, with so many of those present being dedicated researchers and scientists, Satra had virtually a full house, and this heightened the quality of the debates following the well-presented papers.

Georgiana was the first speaker after the morning coffee break. Robin listened diligently to her scholarly presentation. Every now and then their eyes would meet, as he sat in the front row waiting to follow her. He could not help thinking that the voice, the gestures, the easy deportment, were familiar from somewhere. Yet where? It puzzled him throughout her talk, while his attraction for her grew stronger as her erudition impressed him more and more.

Her timing was superb, and as the light on the podium gave a momentary flash to warn the speaker that one more minute was left, the last slide went up.

Robin by then was electrified by all he had heard, and realised that even with his consummate knowledge of the burgeoning subject she would be a difficult act to follow. The applause was tumultuous. The audience had listened to academe at its best in one so young, and no one felt more pride than Robin in the one whose company the day before had given him so much pleasure.

The rest of the day passed as all conferences do - discussions and counter-discussions. Scientific understanding always sparks from the clash of opinions, and Georgiana contributed as much as the others.

At lunchtime Didier came to Robin to seek his judgment on her presentation. He had thought it outstanding.

'She's a high flyer. She'll go far' said Robin.

"She might be a good speaker for the Journées" replied Didier.

'You could do worse. Why don't you go and ask her?'

He watched Didier go over to her and saw her smile as she heard and accepted the invitation. Their eyes met, and he winked at her to show he knew what was going on.

Georgiana wondered whether he had put Didier up to this. For a brief moment she saw a plot, but it was one in which she would only be too glad to be a consenting victim.

'That was a most erudite talk you gave us' Robin told her. 'Congratulations. I learned an awful lot I didn't know. Ken must be very proud of you. '

'Thank you. You are very flattering. You're almost as bad as Didier.'

'No, it isn't flattery. Didier was as impressed as I am. He didn't waste much time deciding to enrol you for the Journées.' Then with a mischievous smile he added 'I told him he could do worse.'

Georgiana laughed heartily at the remark.

'I have some more good news. The Head Concierge has obtained two tickets for the Masked Ball on Saturday.'

Her eyes lit up with pleasure, more so that she knew she would now be spending the last evening of the visit in his company. The way she felt, she would have liked to spend all her evenings with him. Her heart was bubbling with the desire to see as much of him as possible. If only she knew how he felt about her, she thought to herself. She certainly knew how she felt: she was mesmerized by him.

* * * * * * * * *

That afternoon in London, at the General, the Chief Executive had convened an informal discussion involving as many members of the Department of Surgery as he could muster. Since the meeting of the selection committee on the Tuesday evening, the hospital had been in ferment. The fact that no appointment had been made and no formal explanation given had led to much speculation and many unpleasant rumours. There was a feeling that Robin Chesham's decision not to be on the panel might have travelled over the bush telegraph and reached the ears of the Regional Assessor. The junior staff, in turn, were wondering whether some impropriety had taken place, and had asked their spokesman to convey to the CE their concern.

Juniors had been so manipulated in the past, and the demands made on them had been so nefarious, that in all hospitals they had formed their own committees as branches of a national one. In few professions does a career depend so much on the references of so few. The morbid scheming which upholds the rat race to the top had been dubbed the 'three bags full syndrome'. A reference can make or break a career, and such a patronage is a debasing acquiescence of the most outmoded attitude. They felt they wanted to know why this important appointment had not been made, and their demand had caused an explosion which a CE who was inexperienced with such situations could not cope with. Suddenly he needed the help of the senior medical staff. They in turn hardly knew how to handle it.

Medical men are trained neither in politics nor administration, yet many - usually the less clinically able ones - play at being pseudo-politicians and unfledged managers. It is all part of a vain quest for power, or as a smokescreen for their inadequacies. Much of the malaise in the NHS stems from a mixture of the ineptitude of these untutored political parvenus and of second-class unctuous managers.

Frightened by what had happened, and by the suspicion that a situation short of honesty had landed in their laps, these seniors showed themselves to be ineffectual. However inexperienced the CE might have been, he was politically astute. He was after all a political appointment, having previously been a Tory councillor. In the maladroit deportment of the Surgical Department and its fears about the outcome of its behaviour, he saw his chance to reshape the junior staff complement and reduce their number to please his political masters. He therefore decided that an extraordinary meeting of the department be convened ten days hence to address itself to the manner in which appointments were made and to cut down, at the next entry, the number of juniors.

Tom Morgan, Robin's first assistant - in hospital jargon a senior registrar - rang Robin's wife Louise that same evening to apprise her of what had happened and ask her to pass it on to him on his return on the Sunday. He had Robin's confidence, and was not surprised at what had happened.

* * * * * * * *

At the evening meal, Robin and Georgiana found themselves at separate tables. Gustav announced that the gala dinner the next day was scheduled for eight o'clock, and the seating at the tables would be published on the conference notice board by tea-time. Robin caught Georgiana's eyes across the tables as he finished this announcement. They had the same thought.

The dinner over, as the assembly left, Robin cornered Gustav and asked him for a discreet request. It was granted.

The next day, at lunchtime, Robin informed Georgiana that they would both be at table 9 as Gustav's guests. They would also be joined by his research co-worker, Christina Tatio, whose work they both knew. He had also invited Bob Hirst, Didier, Lars Nordin and the president of the local medical society. The radiance on Georgiana's face said it all.

After the last lecture, the delegates went their various ways to return later for the Gala Dinner. Georgiana treated herself to a long, warm shower. Robin found nothing more enjoyable than to soak in a bath perfumed by a Perlier aromatic gel from the generous bottle provided. He was going over the agenda of the satellite meeting of the next day, which Lars was also attending. He would rather have a newspaper to read, but the few English ones had all been snatched. Perhaps he had not got up early enough.

Georgiana knew what she wanted to wear that evening, but was undecided about her underwear. She had spread across the bed a white Harvey Nichols broderie anglaise set made up of a firm bra and comfortable knickers. Alongside, she had stretched a strapless corselet in grey blue lace zipped down most of the middle at the front but elasticised at the back and especially at the top to hold the breasts firmly. It was conveniently fastened at the crotch by unrestricted and easily-undone press studs. She had acquired these items in San Francisco on the occasion of a congress there. She found it very comfortable as it gave her both freedom of movement and sturdy support. She liked wearing it with matching grey-blue tights.

She decided she would keep it to wear the next evening to go to the opera. Perhaps it had subconsciously crossed her mind that it could have certain advantages. That evening she would wear her broderie anglaise set.

Males, luckily, have no such difficulty of choice. They can wear the same suit for most occasions. All they need is a change of briefs or shirts, with perhaps a different tie. Their needs are far less and they can travel light.

Georgiana had decided to wear a pure silk taffeta skirt in deep blue. It was a double-wrap skirt with a single inside button fastening it on the right, while on the left, two outside buttons in a vertical row held it neatly across the waist. Her blouse was of a chic pure chiffon in powder blue. Two panels, crossing over across the front, created a double-breasted high V-neck, the left panel wrapping round the back to be tied to the right one on her left side in a lavish bow.

As Robin got out of the lift in the foyer, he recognised Georgiana by her well-plaited chignon. She had her back to him as she was browsing through the travel brochures and leaflets on the tourist information rack. He went to her.

'Hello.'

When she turned round, he saw the full elegance of what she was wearing.

'You look stunning' he murmured. 'You make me wish I was younger.'

'How nice. Thank you. I don't think age comes into it. I'm afraid you'll have to put up with this again tomorrow evening, as I did not bring an unlimited wardrobe with me.'

'You can dress like this every day as far as I'm concerned. It's a really nice outfit. I do admire your taste.'

Then, realising that perhaps his flattery had been over the top, Robin changed the subject. 'Come on, let's join our host' he said.

Gustav and Christina were already at their table and they were soon joined by their other guests. It was a lavish meal with an unstinting supply of fine wines. The conversation hardly stopped. Over brandy and coffee, Robin enquired if anyone had news of the rest of the world. Gustav had heard rumours that Helsinki might be chosen for a summit conference on the Iraqi situation. Bob Hirst's English newspaper, already 24 hours old, had said that the jury was still out in the Guinness case.

'Integrity seems to be abandoning all walks of life in England' intoned Didier, as if personally outraged. 'It was not like this five years ago when I was there.'

Bob was of the opinion that a policy of greed, giving liberal options and inordinate bonuses to directors and bank executives for pushing profits up rather than improving quality and performance in companies, had created such a climate. In mergers or takeovers much insider manipulation among buddies took place. The outcome of the Guinness case, if it went against the directors involved, would cast a dark shadow on the integrity of the City. There was now a real possibility, by the dawn of the next century, that the 1986 deregulation (the 'Big Bang') in the boardroom and the City in general could lead to a form of admissible corruption, giving directors unacceptable emoluments, options and pensions, to the detriment of the nation's economy and of the less fortunate.

'This does not explain the playful adultery of Ministers, MPs or even royalty' exclaimed Gustav.

'No' said Bob. 'But after ten years in power and with a big majority, boredom sets in and MPs start to stray.'

'I'm not sure this is the full explanation' interrupted Lars. 'Jefferson, Jack Kennedy, Lloyd George - they weren't bored. They abounded in energy. They found themselves away from home frequently and in the constant close association of women on the team. Under such circumstances it would not be hard for them to stray. Furthermore, they had some degree of sexual prowess quite separate from sheer lasciviousness.'

'Is this not a male attitude?' Christina enquired.

Robin now joined in. 'Not really, you have the same attitude in women whether they're queens, top film stars, television personalities or prima ballerinas. No, it isn't gender determined.'

'But all these are people in a position of power!' retorted Christina. 'It's part of their psychology.'

'Psychology is just a word. The psychologists turn an observation into an explanation, and then turn it into a plausible theory' Robin argued. 'You and I, Christina, know all too well that observation must not be confused with explanation. Newton observed gravity, but he didn't explain it. Galileo observed that light must have speed, but he couldn't prove it. I think that in time, with increasing technology, specially in biochemistry, we'll find mental ability and activity have some sort of common mediator with sexual prowess. Then we shall be able to laugh at the psychologists and the psychiatrists with their pseudoscience.'

Didier said he thought there was something wrong with a nation that wallowed in the publicity of the sexual activities of public figures. He had not fully understood that English law enjoyed the hypocrisy of pretending that an Englishman's home is his castle while at the same time allowing the media to invade that privacy. After all, the French knew that their president had a lover and a love child. He had a right to privacy and his private life had nothing to do with his sound governance of the Elysée. He was doing a good job, so what did it matter? The hypothetical argument of the English press that a public man's private behaviour could reflect on his administrative ability was bunkum, and was an easy way of increasing the sale of dubious newspapers through salacious stories.

Lars and Gustav felt the same. The general opinion was that it was time a law of privacy was passed in England, but with so many lawyers making money by defending the indefensible, if not the criminals, no such law was likely to be passed - at least not under the government of the day.

In a world of gender equality, both at work and in domestic life, the old-fashioned concept of adultery was losing its importance in divorce courts, while para-domestic sexual ventures were being tolerated more and more, and need not necessarily bring about the breakdown of an otherwise healthy and companionate relationship.

It was a heated but nonetheless enjoyable discussion, and the concordant views of two professional ladies added to the general consensus. They, however, pointed out how in cases of adultery by their partners, females coped far better than males did and were far more liberal and forgiving in their approach. Furthermore, though they thought that modern feminism was getting out of hand, specially when teasing flirtation at work was being extrapolated into sexual harassment, they made the point that to the male, the current attitude is still that marriage is for sex, whereby many females would look upon sex as not always essential for a contented marriage.

On this note of great sensibility, the group disbanded; but their views were too advanced to receive general acceptance, more so for the many for whom marriage still created physical territorial rights between partners.

CHAPTER SIX

The conference came to an end just before noon on the Saturday. Gustav had organised a buffet lunch to allow those wanting to catch planes or trains to leave as soon as possible. He had asked his speakers to gather in front of the hotel to have a photograph taken of the faculty to be sent as a souvenir of the conference. Either subconsciously or wilfully, Georgiana positioned herself next to Robin. Perhaps she was already eager for closeness.

Two working parties had arranged separate satellite meetings at three o'clock. Georgiana was attending one and Robin the other. They were both planned to end about half past five, and Robin had agreed to call Georgiana soon after a quarter past six, giving him time for a soak in his king-size bath.

When Georgiana's meeting ended soon after five, it seemed a long time to six fifteen. She used the time to go over the protocol agreed at her meeting, then enjoyed a shower and got dressed in readiness for Robin's call. His meeting went well over time, and by twenty past six he had not reached his room. Georgiana was becoming restless by the delay, as the opera started at seven. Her phobia for tardiness was agitating her, when a knock at the door calmed her down.

'I'm sorry to keep you waiting. The usual predicament. Someone was finding problems to every solution.'

'I know the feeling' she smiled.

'You'll have to accept me as I am. I meant to have a bath and change, but there isn't the time. It will take us ten minutes to walk to the Opera House and we have to collect the tickets from the box office.'

In the privacy of the lift he once more remarked on how chic she looked, though he had already observed every detail of her attire the night before. They both felt they were now free from the burden of work. They were already unwinding and looking forward to the evening.

The performance was scintillating. The stage décor, most specially the ballroom, was spectacular and very Swedish. By comparison, the love duet between Riccardo and Amelia was Italian in its romanticism and brought their eyes together as they subconsciously identified with it.

Robin had booked a table at The Boulevardi a few doors away, a haunt of artists and many of the opera performers. Indeed, a short while after they had sat down, a group from the Opera House occupied a larger table close to theirs.

The production naturally occupied part of Robin and Georgiana's conversation, and Georgiana raised the comparison with La Traviata. Whereas in the latter the lovers meet in comfort, can express their feelings in privacy and consummate their love in opulent surroundings, this was not the case in Un Ballo in Masquera. Amelia's love for Riccardo is a desperate and disorderly one, while his love for her has greater nobility than Alfredo's for Violeta. Amelia is torn by remorse and fear, and there is almost a physical fever in their love duet. It is unparalleled in any of Verdi's work and is comparable to Wagner's treatment of the redemption of love in Tristan and Isolde, an opera they both knew.

The conversation was not all serious. When Robin said the original Dame aux Camélias had worn a white flower as a means of telling her lovers about her physiological availability, Georgiana retorted: 'At my boarding school, we knew about the off-limits days when the older girls wore black knickers!'

'Well' laughed Robin. 'Traviata was clearly more discreet!'

While they were having coffee, Robin leaned conspiratorially across the table. 'I hope that what I am going to tell you will not offend you' he said.

Georgiana looked puzzled for a split second.

'I'll tell you if it does' she replied.

'I have fallen in love with you.'

'Snap' she murmured. She placed her right hand across the table towards him, palm up, inviting his. He placed his left one over it and gently held it.

'This has not happened to me for over twenty-five years. What do you think we should do about it?' he asked.

'I'll leave that to you' she replied.

'I have a bottle of champagne in my room. I think we should go up and open it. To celebrate.'

Georgiana's eyes were wider than ever as she quickly brought up her left hand to cover her nose as she sneezed twice.

As they walked back, the tender light of an almost full moon, half way up in a thin, fleecy southern sky, kissed the side of Georgiana's forehead. It canopied her eyes as every now and then a fleeting small wispy cloud would veil the moonlight from her face. In this quivering glimmer she seemed still more attractive and alluring to him.

'I feel like putting my arm around you, but we could be seen and that would compromise you' he said. She nodded her agreement, though she wanted the arm very much.

'I'll put the bottle on ice when we get back. Would you mind if I had a quick bath first, and then call you?'

'Good plan' said Georgiana. She wanted to freshen up too.

Robin clicked on the corner light as he walked into his room. He placed two flutes in the fridge, moved the champagne bottle into the bucket over the bar and placed some ice around it. He pushed into his Dictaphone a cassette of a medley of tunes and songs, and switched it on. The curtain had been drawn and the bed cover pulled back by the chambermaid earlier on. He ran a bath, stripped quickly and then dropped into it with relish.

In her room, Georgiana felt exhilarated. She kicked off her shoes as if she wanted to float up into the air, and made for the bathroom. It was heated by a large electric towel rail, and was very warm.

Sitting there, meditating over the last part of the evening, she became unsure about what Robin meant by 'celebrate'. She was burning with the desire to be possessed. She knew that if it did not happen that evening, it might never happen. That notion did not appeal to her.

She pulled off her tights, combed her hair, remembered to take her pill and went back to her room, pacing it with impatience. He would put all his clothes back on after his bath, she was certain. Such a simple thing could spoil it all.

A woman's impulse for passion is no different from the male's. It is a matter of culture that the first move is meant to come from the male, but the receptiveness is essentially a female prerogative; and receptive she had become.

She thought again about what that word 'celebrate' meant. Was it going to be just this? Some inherent instinctive force gained mastery over her. She decided to act.

With eyes closed, listening to the music from the bedroom, relaxing in his bath and absorbed in thoughts about Georgiana, Robin was awakened by a double knock at his door. Shit! What idiot wanted to talk business to him so late in the evening?

He jumped out of the bath, quickly put his bathrobe on, tied the belt and went to open the door. It was Georgiana.

'Sorry, am I too early?' she said, struggling to keep a serious face. 'It's OK, I'll come back later.'

'No! I'm delighted' said Robin. 'I thought it was one of the chaps. Do come in. I hope you don't mind me as I am.'

He moved from the door to let her in, and she sneezed again.

'Sit down. The bubbly should be just right. Turn the music off if it isn't to your taste.'

'No problem, I love it' she said.

He did the honours, two-thirds filled a flute, handed it to her, then poured himself some. Then he noticed that her legs and feet were bare.

'How sensible of you to be unshod' he said. 'The floors are so warm to the feet, they must have underfloor heating.' He had rather missed the point; she had been trying to look sexy.

The champagne flowed, and they began to talk. She remarked how spacious his room was and how pleasing the colour scheme. There was also a youthful sensuousness about the furnishing, which the wide curtains, in the same fabric, enhanced.

'They're very thick' he said. 'They blot out the halogen street lights, thank goodness. But when you open them, the view of the waterfront and the city beyond is quite splendid.'

He took her to the window, drew apart the curtains, and pointed out to her the gardens on the other side of the water and the small islands guarding the entrance to the bay. A ship was passing slowly by on its way in to the harbour.

Robin was standing close behind her. The light, musky scent of the perfume she was wearing was heightened by the sweet scent of her own flesh. The combination provoked a carnal longing in him. He put both arms around her, clasping his hands in front of her, and leaned his head over her left shoulder.

'I have been longing to do this' he said. 'I just didn't want to be too forward.'

'I wish you had' she replied, turning to face him. 'I've been longing as well.' Her eyes were shining. With her head tilted backwards and her mouth half open, she offered him her lips.

His left hand held her tightly to him as he pressed his lower body firmly against hers. She could feel him harden perceptibly. A warm sensation invaded her entire body.

With his right hand, he undid the bow that fastened her blouse, then popped open the two outer buttons of her skirt and finally the inner one. It dropped to the floor. Without interrupting their kiss, he removed her blouse. Then he gently lifted her, carried her to the bed and laid her upon it. As he unzipped her corselet, her left breast was revealed, exposing a pink crinkled areola and an erect nipple which was begging to be sucked. As he did so she clasped her hands around his head to keep it there. His right hand moved to her thighs, and she spread her legs wide. He found the press-studs that fastened it and popped them open. His hand explored her and his fingers invaded her. She let her hands fall from his head. More and more aroused, she rolled her head from side to side across the pillow with frenzied pleasure.

His wetted fingers now became conscious of that tumescence which is at the same time solicitous and consentient. He stood away from her to disrobe, and as he did so she pulled her corselet off in one swift movement.

As he lay over her, she drew up both legs with thighs wide open as he lost himself within her. Their lips met again and they worked in unison, shifting their bodies from side to side and constantly changing position, unhurriedly, while offering each other time to relish the sensations of their lovemaking. Neither rushed the other's peak. At last Georgiana, sitting astride him, quickened her movements towards her own climax. He suddenly felt that contraction which heralded the divine moment. He responded with accelerated, deeper movements, driving her to bury her head in the pillow. It did little to muffle her paroxysm of delight as they reached simultaneously the acme of their passion, drenching each other in climax.

The music on the cassette player was still playing. As they reached the last moments of their passion, the final strains of Lara's Theme from Dr Zhivago were fading with their own climax. It was a coincidence that it was a favourite of his, but they would remember it forever.

As their ardour died down they rolled on to their sides, their breathless bodies still tightly yoked together, still engorged with pleasure, and drifted into a deep, semi-wakeful repose. Robin reached for the light switch to bring a partial darkness to the room. Together they sank into unconsciousness.

Deep in the night, it was the unfamiliar warmth of the bed that woke Robin. He was looking at the numbers 444 fluorescing in green, and for a moment he wondered what it meant, until the third numeral changed to a five and he realised it was the digital clock on the TV set. Georgiana's profile, illuminated by the reflected glare of the street lights, looked peaceful and contented. He watched it for a while, feeling an intense desire to caress her, trespass on her sleep and repossess her body. Then he decided that it would be selfish to disturb so much tranquillity and connubial bliss. He went back to sleep.

The satiny light of a day-break sun spilled into the room through the window; the curtains were still drawn back from the night before. He looked at Georgiana curled on to her right side, still lulled by the ebbing tide of sleep that the dawn had not yet disturbed.

He wanted her. He wanted more. He drew himself closer to her until his thighs engaged her buttocks. She moved, realised where she was and pressed her back into him. She moved still tighter against him, drew up her knees, laid herself open to him, and gave a grunt of delight as she felt him take her. After some moments she drew away enough to turn on to her back and welcome him face to face.

'Good morning to you, Mr Chesham' she smiled. He thought he had never seen such a beautiful face, now so drowned in love and sex.

It was broad daylight when they finally broke away from each other's panting gratification, their lips still burning from the last moment of disengagement. He lay motionless, peacefully cradled within her thighs, his head pillowed upon her left shoulder.

He must have fallen asleep in that position with his weight over her left arm, numbing it and forcing her to pull it away from under him. He woke up at the sensation.

'I'm sorry' he said. 'Am I maiming you?'

'No, but my arm was getting a bit numb.'

He looked at the digital clock. It was well gone nine.

'Golly! I have monopolised you for far longer than you may have wanted.'

'I'm not complaining. I can't think of anything nicer than being here.'

They smiled at each other and agreed it was time to get up.

He was standing at the toilet when she came into the bathroom, looked at herself in the mirror and started pulling back her tangled hair.

'Do you want me to leave?' she said.

'Don't be silly' he laughed. 'I have nothing to hide from you now.'

'OK.'

It was her turn to use the loo. As she sat on it Robin could not help teasing her in return.

'Do you want me to leave?' he simpered at her. She stuck her tongue out at him. He bent gently over her and kissed her forehead.

He suggested that she should stay, have a bath in his suite and use the guest toothbrush and comb. Neither of them were too bothered about breakfast. A generous squirt of bath gel produced a richly-scented pink foam, and Georgiana was soon buried under it.

'That looks nice' he said. 'Can I join you?'

'Why not?'

'I hope you don't feel I took advantage of you last night' he said.

'I seem to remember that I was the one who knocked on the door and invited herself in when you were in the bath' she responded.

Robin smiled. 'By the way, I must reassure you about any untoward consequences' he said. 'I have had the snip.'

'Don't worry, I'm well protected. I wouldn't have taken the risk, I can assure you.'

'Of course. Sorry I raised it.'

'You certainly did that' she grinned.

Robin had not intended a one-night stand and he was determined that the previous night would not turn into one. He knew he had fallen in love again; this could be no mere infatuation. He felt sure they would meet again many times and find themselves enraptured by the same desires.

He was now in the strange situation of being in love with two women, knowing one love would not displace the other. He quizzed Georgiana about her own feelings and found that she was as attached to her partner and her home as he was to his. She had not expected to encounter this new passion. She was now having to grapple with two mutually-exclusive ways of being sexually gratified, and she needed time to translate this into two different sets of emotions which she could live with side by side. Intellectually she would certainly find a way of rationalising her behaviour, but the truth was that she had been struck by lightning.

She had yet to understand, unlike Robin, how she could have come to be part of him with so much alacrity. It was an eagerness that had taken her by surprise and for which, as yet, she had no explanation.

He, on the other hand, had fallen in love twice before. He knew the symptoms, and he knew what a powerful emotion it is, how all-embracing it could be, and how it tends to exclude everything else. There were two Robins, and one of them was with her. His mind was not split, but the emotions of one Robin were very different from those of the other. He was not going to tell her about all this, because he knew that women are always distressed by comparisons, and anyway he had too great a sense of innate privacy to discuss past experiences with others.

She got out of the bath first, and as she moved to the washbasin she could see Robin in the mirror with a smile on his face.

'What are you smiling about?'

'Your bottom moves just like a swan. Very enjoyable.'

'So I'm a swan now!'

'May be it would be better if I were the swan and you were Leda.'

She laughed at the thought.

To both of them, it was not so much a question of squaring a circle. Their intellects allowed them to understand what they were feeling for each other. From a state of emotional contemplation, they had now moved into one of predictive reality, of knowing that they would be meeting frequently in circumstances that would rekindle their feelings and reactivate their passion. Perhaps they should meet away from such situations, and see whether time and distance would make them feel differently. But the now of this moment could be a now that would repeat itself over and over again, and leave in them an awareness of a sense of the forever.

' You said that Wednesdays were your free days' said Georgiana. 'I'm at a meeting in Newbury on the 26th of September. Could we meet after that?'

Georgiana was planning to visit her parents in Henley that

afternoon, but there would be time for them to spend a few hours together in between. Robin suggested the French Horn in Sonning, and Georgiana, who knew it well, jumped at the idea.

She borrowed the guest bathrobe to get back to her room; it would have looked very strange to be seen in evening dress at eleven in the morning. She could come back for her clothes and pack before noon, when they had to be out of their rooms.

After lunch they visited the west side of the peninsula. The few hours left to them seemed to pass very quickly.

It was a quarter past seven when they got out of the terminal building at London Airport. Margaret had come to meet him. It was a short distance from her home in Hounslow and she had been looking after his Rolls while he was away. He suggested taking Georgiana to the Heathrow Royal after he had driven Margaret home. It would give them a little longer together.

Once they were on their own again, she asked him about the car.

'I bought it for a song when everyone had cold feet about the oil crisis of the early seventies' he said. 'It was useful tax-wise then, but now that the top rate is so much lower, it is no longer tax efficient. It is also grossly overrated, like the Spanish School in Vienna. My Toyota is far more reliable, though strangely enough, the insurance on the Roller is cheaper. Anyone driving a Roller is supposed to be a careful driver, so you get a lower premium.'

At the hotel, their parting kisses had a tinge of sadness to them. Robin comforted himself by remembering that he could reach Georgiana at work on the phone any time he wanted to, and she could do likewise with him at the General.

He felt the heavy heart of parting as he watched her disappear into the hotel. As he turned the Rolls on to the A4 the skies had turned grey and it had started raining, and suddenly the splendour of the day seemed to have died.

He could not get Georgiana out of his mind until he had reached

Baker Street and was heading towards Regent's Park. Then his mood suddenly changed. He found his old self again, and began to look forward to being home.

Georgiana did not reach Bath until long after Robin had arrived at his house in The Avenue. Her whole journey was spent reliving the events of Helsinki. Her husband wanted to know all about the meeting, but she did not feel like telling him. She blamed her tiredness for her reticence. She was still too close to the events of the preceding night to unwind completely. She needed the night to calm her down.

* * * * * * * *

As Robin drove up his gravelled drive, the crunching noise of the car's tyres had brought Cio-Cio, their seventeen-year-old brown Burmese cat, to the porch. She loved welcoming her owners home. She knew their footsteps and the sound of their respective cars and she would always be there to greet them. When Robin opened the door, Cio-Cio had to be the first in. She always took precedence over everybody else.

It was gone nine, and Louise had been impatient to see him. She had changed into her long pink muslin housecoat, and through the diaphanous mesh her naked body was discernible. She was just as he wanted her to be. He was home. He was with her.

As they walked upstairs to the bedroom, Cio-Cio's muffled special miaow - vocalising her feline discernment of smells - told them that she was carrying something down; the knickers Louise had taken off earlier. Cio-Cio was giving her master the all-clear. As for Robin, he could not wait to make love to Louise.

Much later they came downstairs again, and Louise gave him all the messages that had arrived in his absence - especially the one about the débâcle at the General. It was more than he had expected, but deep inside he felt his judgment had been right.

CHAPTER SEVEN

The General Hospital Medical School, like all its kind, had too few beds to provide adequate teaching facilities for its intake of students. It had therefore, many years previously, co-opted the North Poplar District General Hospital to increase its training amenities in Medicine, Surgery and Obstetrics and Gynaecology. There were three or four units or 'firms' per discipline, each under the personal aegis of an autonomous consultant. This had been established since the start of the NHS, which had totally altered the structure of health care as it had existed before the Labour government of Clement Attlee. It had been a government of compassion, which removed from medical care the worry of cost and offered healthcare free of charge at the point of need. Insurance contributions and taxes had been the main source of its eventually inadequate funding.

During the war years of the early forties the defence of the nation had been firmly entrusted to Winston Churchill, but the task of looking ahead to rebuilding a better Britain once the war had been won was left to a coalition government under the overall control of Attlee. In the pre-war years, medical education, for the most part, stopped with obtaining a qualification at a final examination. Everything that needed to be known was deemed to have been acquired during the undergraduate years. Only a few stayed in the hospital environment to obtain higher qualifications, and most of these were in the teaching hospitals. The consultants there were prima donnas. The students stood in awe in their presence and were expected, once qualified and in general practice, to refer to them patients for treatment, preferably privately.

With the rapid and continuing advances in medical knowledge it had become obvious to the Attlee administration that a qualifying examination was only the beginning, and that true training could start only after qualification. This principle had been enunciated in the Goodenough Report of 1943 and was to be the basis of the Labour Government Medical Acts of 1951, requiring all graduates to spend a year of training in house appointments in hospital posts before obtaining a licence or registration to practise.

Over the years, the provincial cities had founded their own universities or medical schools, rivalling more and more the old-fashioned metropolitan institutions. The names of saints given to the latter had created an air of godliness that they did not always live up to. The 'Saint' part was often dropped; thus the products of St Bartholomew's, for example, were referred to as Bart's graduates. Some medical schools were hallmarked by various extramural activities, and if you were a great rugby player you might find a niche at St Mary's. There was also a degree of arrogance in some. It was frequently said that that you could always tell a Bart's man when you saw one, but you could not tell him anything.

The alma mater and the 'old school tie' created a patronage of their own. If public schools had bought influence and power through inherited wealth - and the children of the aristocracy were not interested in the menial profession of medicine - the grammar schools and comprehensives were creating a meritocracy based on assessment of intelligence, as a means of breaking up the traditional English class barriers. On the other hand, the professional classes were becoming snobs who believed that their children would have better opportunities in the future if they spent vast sums - often beyond their means - sending them to private schools of dubious merit.

Until state schools improved their standards, that reasoning had much to support it. As a result, a degree of selfish selectivity started to pervade society, and in the early days it crept into the ethos of some medical schools. The educational equality propounded by such thinkers as Locke was being eroded by the belief that the home, or an élitist school habitat, would transcend inherited intelligence, while psychologists were determined, without scientific evidence, to support the idea that genes were less important than environment.

As medical schools started to increase their intake of female students, the two genders were being thrown together more and more for at least five years at university level, with the result that marriages of intelligence were becoming more frequent than marriages of background. A new aristocracy of inherited genes was producing its own meritocratic offspring. Given time, a new generation with centre political views would replace extreme right or extreme left political thought and the country, like Europe, would become less partisan in its socio-economic philosophy.

However, the atmosphere in teaching hospitals and in the medical profession remained, as a whole, fairly parochial. This attitude prevailed in the sixties and seventies and was still influencing the eighties. The General and the North Poplar hospitals had not yet moved into an egalitarian or socially-just attitude of mind, and there was an old brigade which still believed in furtive activities, in jealousies, and in the constant quest for self-seeking power. Yet, the NHS had created the very atmosphere that removed egocentricity from medicine. The pyramidal system of old had been replaced by a plateau where all consultants were to be paid equally, would benefit from a good standard of life and would not have to behave like rival tradesmen.

Such theoretical equality did not meet the approval of the power-hungry. How could men who were forever enlarging the horizons of medicine or translating their ideas into therapeutic actions be remunerated similarly to those who were content to have an easy life and take no interest in spearheading new advances? The leaders needed to be rewarded for their achievements or efforts. The concept of distinction or merit awards was created to achieve this, but it all had to be secret, openness being an alien concept of officialdom, more so medical officialdom. Such an award was a sum paid in addition to one's salary for the rest of one's professional life and would enhance one's pension. It paid handsomely to be a beneficiary of such a bounty.

The profession had thereby offered the politicians an ideal means of dividing its august body into the haves and the have nots - an act of slow destruction which could create only rivalry, mistrust, dishonesty and eventually a self-meted out deregulation of the medical profession, with, worst of all, a covert system of benefaction.

Technically, under English Law, everyone is equal; above all there should be no race or gender discrimination. Sociologically, however, this so-called 'justice' is yet to be achieved by an out-of-date legal system. Justice remains tarred with the brush of patronage and prejudice. Both mean serfdom.

Patronage always carries an obligation which is expected to be lifelong. Patronage is the bait. Obligation is the hook. Neither recognises loyalty.

The loose amalgamation of The General and the North Poplar; the furtive manipulation of these awards; the crave for power by the less able clinical members; all created in that merger of two unequal hospitals a climate in which ambivalent personalities were constantly genuflecting in front of the altar of political ambition or the shrine of avarice. Every hospital has evolved such men and they, more than anything else, were to be the wreckers of the NHS.

In this hallowed halcyon time a gust of political change was blowing, whipped up by untested principles and gyrated by an essentially doctrinaire vortex. The NHS was to be 'reformed', except that no one quite knew what the word implied. The fashion that year, 1990, was for refashioning - but as what? The in word had become the 'internal market', with buyers and sellers. Medicine would be a commodity based not on need but on the supply of money. This would mean rationing by brainless controllers with no understanding of priorities.

The General had applied to be in the first wave of the formation of Trust Hospitals and had been successful. Every head of a department would therefore carry the grandiose name of director.

A Chief Executive had been appointed. By sheer coincidence he was an active member of the local Conservative Party. It was an appointment that would have indirectly pleased the attitude of mind of the grocer's daughter of Downing Street. He was to replace the reigning chairman of the Hospital Health Authority, himself appointed three years previously by the powers-that-be from a brick-making company. He understood the business of demand and supply, but in terms of medicine, or indeed the human body, he did not know his elbow from his arse. He had been a dismal failure.

There were those, however, who saw it as to their advantage to curry favour with him. Among them was Ian Cook, one of the lesser surgeons. His name had been recommended to the CE by the departing chairman, and it was no surprise when he was made the first Medical Director of the newly established Trust. This certainly carried some degree of power, patronage and opportunity for political intrigues, and could well buy the incumbent a merit award. It was a sought-after position.

Ian Cook was a stocky, even podgy, Glaswegian of limited academic ability. Indeed he was somewhat proud of his ignorance of scientific methods in the pursuit of medical advances. He sported a reddish beard hiding a weak chin. In spite of being a medical man he would smoke a pipe, not infrequently an empty one, reflecting perhaps his general meanness and perhaps his Scottish thriftiness, to which was grafted a strange display of Presbyterian fundamentalism, as long as its principles did not apply to him. He should have remained a big fish in a small pool; instead he found himself, by accident through his appointment at the North Poplar, to be a small fish in a big pond. He had therefore to strive constantly at pretending to be big.

He had graduated from his home university - just. Then he had striven hard to take a higher surgical qualification. He had failed frequently, but colleges and universities were still doing well out of these failures. It was, at the time, a good steady source of funds, and somehow such flounderings were tolerated.

Eventually he obtained a surgical Fellowship from his local college, and by dint of effort - which was commendable - managed that of the Edinburgh College, but had never been able to meet the requirements of the same grade south of the Border. However, his failures were too well known locally for him to progress and he had emigrated to the anonymity of London, where he had slowly crept up the mid-rungs of a ladder with convergent uprights and obtained a consulting appointment at North Poplar District General Hospital. He had been given a dozen or so in-patient beds, but his main role was to supervise the Casualty Department which, at the North Poplar, ran a varicose ulcer clinic as well as one dealing with anal fissures and haemorrhoids. Here Cook became known as the Bum Doctor. As his surgical colleagues retired one by one, he acquired some of their clinical sessions, a common practice in those days, and eventually managed to offload his casualty duties. The merger with the General allowed him to apply the same principles there, and he soon poached three sessions at that hospital. He had arrived.

After having professed a specialised interest in rectal surgery for some 20 years he had, through friends at court, obtained an honoris causa diploma of the remaining college. His headed paper was a collection of re-echoing letters which were meaningless to the public but good for his ego.

His middle names were Campbell and Mackenzie. After becoming a consultant he had hyphenated his name to Mackenzie-Cook. It made him feel good - superior. It was snobbism shoring up ineptitude. It was pretension coming to the rescue of the inadequate. He liked dropping names and even claimed some relationship to the Dukes of Argyll - or at least to the Campbell clan. He felt a great necessity to claim such a proud degree of genetic cronyism, and in the same vein he believed that belonging to the proper club, or hunting and fishing with titled people, or inviting the local practitioners to champagne parties, gave him distinction.

On formal occasions he would wear a kilt, sometimes of the Campbells, sometimes of the Mackenzies, depending on the purpose of the function. He wore with them a magnificent sporran, a symbolic fig leaf that was a good cover for many shortcomings.

The General had in common with many similar institutions the particularity that those lacking clinical or academic brilliance would hide their failings by sitting on every ongoing committee and frequently offering to chair them. It gave them an aura of importance, if not of power, but it was a power by default through their colleagues not being prepared to devote some of their time to such suspicious pursuits. These arrivés remained oblivious of the scornful words of their colleagues, and anyway would be too thick-skinned to feel hurt by them. Nonetheless, they served a purpose, if not necessarily that of the long-term good of their hospital.

For administrative purposes, the North Poplar was eventually placed under the umbrella of the General, with its incumbent specialists having a place on the latter's many committees. This state of affairs had allowed Ian Cook to worm his way into as many committees as he could, and eventually he had offered himself as Chairman of the Appointments Committee. Such self-appointment is not without hubris, and not without perverted power, if not unscrupulousness.

Until self-regulation and self-procurement is taken away from the medical profession, this climate will prevail. It is not likely to be altered by a right-wing government with appointed chums at all levels. Sooner or later the bubble will burst, and then it will be too late for the profession to recover from the self-inflicted wounds of its past. But the prevailing climate well suited the likes of Ian Cook.

He had married young, into new money, a nurse in his local hospital. She was the daughter of a local bricklayer-cum-builder who, in the years following the devastation of the war, had made quick money in his trade. He had then opened his own estate agency, which had coined it for him. He was rich but not wealthy. He took pleasure in splashing out and showered on his only child the outward manifestations of money. Born in that humble milieu in the late thirties, she fell heir to the expected and unimaginative names of Florence Olga - Flo to her friends. Junior staff had unkindly baptised her 'Mrs FOC'. Money had made her pretentious without giving her the savoir faire. They were a complementary couple, and she was no doubt extremely proud of her husband being so much in demand on so many committees and would tell all her friends about it.

However, the events of the previous week at the Appointments Committee must have weighed heavily on the mind of her husband during the absence from the country of his most dreaded colleague.

* * * * * * * * *

Robin Chesham was in his office at the General shortly before 8.30 am. There was a note marked 'urgent' from Ian Cook asking to come and see him at 12.30.

Robin had a ward round that morning, starting at nine and usually finishing by noon. His hospital secretary had already pencilled the request in his diary. Robin agreed to it.

Soon after, Tom Morgan called in to update Robin on events since the previous Tuesday. Most of the junior staff were recent appointees, and they were the first intake of fresh graduates under the new Trust. They were appalled at the rumours that under the new régime there appeared already to be some shilly-shallying, and this had affected their morale. In addition it was mooted that the re-appointment of the senior registrar would be postponed for some six months as a face saver for those involved in the hash of the previous week. This was useful information in the light of Ian Cook's request to see Robin later that morning.

'How do your colleagues see this mess?' Robin asked Tom.

'The senior registrars are in an angry mood. If something underhand really has taken place, they feel it demeans their status. In terms of the rotation system, a delay of six months in an appointment would upset the natural flow of the rotation. They would prefer the post to be re-advertised immediately.'

'I appreciate their feelings. I also agree with their views, but re-advertising the post will only create bad publicity. We need some diplomacy. We need to cut those who are responsible for this shambles down to size. Some horse-trading may be needed. We need to exact from them as a face-saver a demand for an honest way of choosing candidates, or even a more equitable way of shortlisting applicants. We also need to remove from the present practice any vested interest or privilege.'

Tom said he followed this argument, but hammered home his colleagues' disapproval of what they were hearing.

'How has Bacon taken this?' Robin asked.

'He is very upset and depressed. He feels he is now in a crossfire situation that may badly reflect on his career, through no fault of his.'

'Yes, he's going to need help. All this will make it more difficult to find a niche for him in the near future. He has been the victim of manipulators.'

They carried on the conversation on the way to the wards for the unit's ward round, which took place in an atmosphere of friendly informality, as if nothing had happened the week before. As was his usual custom, Robin and his team were joined by the Nursing Officer and the charge nurses for coffee, a practice that allowed a free discussion about the various clinical problems on the unit, with everyone concerned having an equal say regardless of status. It was a forum for an open exchange of views, something to which Robin attached great importance.

* * * * * * * * *

Ian Cook arrived on time. At least he knew how to use a watch. Perhaps it was the Presbyterian indoctrination in his upbringing, but this equated badly with his tinkering mentality.

'Did you have a good meeting?' he enquired of Robin, to break the ice.

'Yes, thank you. It was most informative and very well run. It was also very enjoyable. Far more enjoyable than what happened here, I gather.'

'You can say that again! We were subjected to a lot of flak on the Appointments Committee. That's what I wanted to discuss with you.'

Robin did not take up the cue. 'It's being suggested that we re-advertise in six months to let the dust settle' Cook went on.

Robin volunteered that he had heard much about what happened and was not interested in hearing chapter and verse on what was said.

'I wouldn't go along with that' he said. 'Before we go any further, I want to know how the candidates were finally chosen. My shortlist picked what I considered the four best out of some twenty applicants. Out of courtesy to Bacon, as a local candidate, I included him, though I felt he was not in the same class as many of the others.'

'There was a wide scatter in the short listing with little overlap, so Bob decided on the final names' replied Cook. Bob was the Professor of Surgery.

'But surely it was not for Bob to decide on his own?'

'Well, he discussed it with me and I felt that this was as good as we could expect.'

'Why can't we reselect from the list of the original applicants?'

'There's a problem here. It seems that we had all binned the other CVs once the short-listed candidates had agreed to present themselves. The Director of Human Resources had done the same. So we no longer have access to their names and CVs.'

'That's rather strange. But I may still have them' he said. Ian Cook's face fell.

Robin went to his filing cabinet and saw that the CVs were indeed all there. But realising that he was holding a trump card, he pretended not to have found them. He registered the sudden calm that returned to Cook's face.

'I shall check up at home' he went on. 'So what's next?'

Ian Cook informed him that a meeting had been arranged for the next Monday over lunch to discuss the question of a postponement and a reorganisation of the junior staff complement, as proposed by the CE. Robin made it clear that he would not agree to a cut in the number of juniors, but requested a full and precise agenda so that the meeting would be of a statutory nature with all decisions binding. He did not mince his words. He wanted the mess about the shortlist sorted out without equivocation.

'This nonsense of having devolved our contracts from the Regional Authority to the Trust is already showing that local manipulation might have taken place' he said. 'I do not go along with the way directors are going to put the Trust's interests before those of the juniors or the patients. I'm surprised you appear to go along with the possibility of lesser men being appointed. This system will emasculate the profession.'

Ian Cook left him looking crestfallen and feared the worst. He was very aware that Robin Chesham was not a man who could be bought, and he was not looking forward to the meeting. Furthermore, Robin had given him no clear indication as to what he had in mind, so he was not in a position to start scheming. This was precisely why Robin was playing his cards close to his chest. He too could play that game.

* * * * * * * *

Robert Randall had been in the Chair of Surgery for five years. He was not especially outstanding as a scientist, but he did have the gift of bringing himself down to the level of the students and as such was a good teacher - an essential attribute in a teaching hospital in which so many have never been trained to teach, and for some reason are expected to know it instinctively. At the time of his appointment there had been an acute shortage of suitable candidates for a Chair.

Bob Randall had been a lecturer in surgery at the General, and had previously been Senior Registrar to a Mr Archibald Bacon, who enjoyed flattery and had been instrumental in him getting the Chair of Surgery. Bacon had long since passed away. He had been a relic of the early days of the NHS, when as the eldest surgical 'honorary' he had insisted on being called Senior Surgeon. By then the NHS had toppled the pyramidal structure of hospital hierarchy and had brought all consultants to the same level. There were many who had found this hard to stomach, and Archibald Bacon had held on to his out-of-date prestige until retirement.

Bob Randall's father had spent heavily on educating his son at one of London's expensive public schools. Once appointed to the Chair of Surgery, Bob had decided covertly that he would only appoint juniors who had been educated at public schools, as he deemed them the most promising candidates. This policy had not gone unnoticed in the hospital. By comparison Robin Chesham had kept a ledger of all the juniors trained under him and had continued to follow their careers. He held that state schools eventually produced graduates who showed greater potential than the public-school-educated ones, probably because the latter had been spoon fed to pass exams and by the time they reached university were mentally exhausted. He appointed his juniors not from where they had been educated but for what they had achieved since and were likely to go on achieving. He wanted them also to be able to relate with ease to their patients and their colleagues, be they nursing or medical, proving themselves to be good doctors - a policy different from that of the Professor. His appointments were thus a very mixed group.

As Archibald Bacon's son Colin had also been to a public school and read Medicine at the General's Medical School, he had, not unexpectedly, become a protégé of the Professor's. There was in this a sense of obligation, if not actually a deep-seated wish to be loyal, and perhaps a realisation of having been rescued from the possibility of academic oblivion.

The young Bacon was no luminary. He needed patronage. He had bought this by accepting a research appointment to carry out work on markers in pre-cancerous states, something the Professor was keen on. It did not matter whether he had any ability to carry out such work, or even the vaguest interest in it. He knew he had to do something to stay in the rat race. He had, after all, been 'brought up well' at his school and appreciated the advantages of hypocrisy.

He had held his first appointment as a house physician in the Department of Gastroenterology to which Robin belonged. It was one of the few departments of its type in the country, in that it was run jointly by a physician and a surgeon, who shared the same wards and joint out-patient facilities and did ward rounds together once a week with a team made up of dedicated radiologists, pathologists and juniors. Colin Bacon had been the house officer to Robin's physician counterpart, Dr John Gammon, who unfortunately had been disappointed with his performance. Often a first post can be daunting and the incumbent must not be too harshly judged at such an early stage. Colin Bacon had decided on a surgical career; he had taken the first part of his surgical fellowship and had moved slowly up the ranks.

Halfway through Bacon's research appointment the Professor had asked Robin to be an assessor and look at the young man's work. Robin had studied it carefully and had to point out that it was flawed. But it was too late to recast the the whole protocol, and imperfect as it was, it had to continue. Somehow a thesis of sorts would be excavated from it. Robin felt he could not go along with this and politely withdrew from being an assessor. He was equally protecting his name from being linked with an unacceptable thesis that would confer a degree. Such, at times, are the machinations of events in a system with imperfections. Unless there was an effort at correcting the obvious distortions in the self-regulation of the profession, sooner or later it would have to be regulated by the State. Many realised this, and Robin was among those pressing for a major change in attitude to avoid state interference.

This was the climate in which an unfortunate appointment had not taken place and in which a contentious meeting was to be held a week later. It would be a long week for many, above all Bacon himself, who was hoping that a six-month postponement of an appointment could work in his favour.

* * * * * * * * *

As half past one approached, Robin went to the public phone box in the Medical School and rang Bath. He had promised to call Georgiana, and that time of the day was for her the most propitious moment.

The sound of her voice dissipated from his mind the gloom of the political manoeuvres that were going on, and he was relieved to hear that she had a reasonable journey back and had not been too overwrought by the emotional events of the previous day. He found her in a happy state of mind, equally pleased to hear from him and hoping on a reunion sooner rather than later. It put him in a joyous mood, and he almost danced his way back to the operating theatre for his afternoon session.

In the weeks that followed they kept in touch with each other in various ways. Usually Robin rang her from his rooms. He agreed to try and meet her on the Wednesday she had suggested and at the restaurant Robin had proposed. They could have been young lovers on a first rapture of emotion, so keen were they to see each other.

* * * * * * * * *

The remainder of the week was a busy one for Robin, as is always the case whenever time is taken off to attend a conference - so much so that many consultants choose to attend as few as they can, often on the pretext that they have too many NHS commitments when they really mean that they are too engrossed in their private work. Though Robin Chesham had an active private practice, he had decided early in his career that his home life and his research interests would come first and he limited his private work to Wednesdays, though he would always visit his privately-operated patients on his way home in the evening. His NHS work always took precedence and he would operate privately before nine in the morning or after his day's work at the General only if it were an emergency. It was therefore difficult to fault him. This allowed him to be openly critical of what he saw. Often he was accused of being over-critical, but this never bothered him.

CHAPTER EIGHT

The lunchtime meeting the following week was animated, even acrimonious. Robin had been in touch with those who had been asked to send in their own shortlists and he had carefully studied them and tabulated them. He had come to the conclusion that contrary to what Ian Cook had told him, there had been enough overlap of choice for a different shortlist to have been worked out. He had photocopied this table, as well as the CVs of all applicants, and had enough copies run off for distribution to all those who would attend the meeting.

Ian Cook, chairing it in his role as Medical Director, gave a lengthy explanation about what had happened and how the shortlist was arrived at.

Robin moved in for a fight straight away.

'Am I correct in saying that you and Bob drew the shortlist on the grounds that there was too great a scatter in the choices you received, and concluded that the fairest choice was the one you arrived at?'

'That's how I saw it' Cook replied.

'And this was after conferring with Bob and no one else, I gather?'

'That's right.'

'May I then pass round a table showing how the other surgeons who contributed a requested shortlist had voted. Somehow, it seems to me that the final choice was, to say the least, myopic.'

Once the table had been studied by all present, Robin continued: 'You can see that there was in fact far more overlap than we are led to believe, and that a very different shortlist should have been arrived at.'

A silence met this argument.

Bob Randall muttered a few irrelevant points that Robin did not accept. When he challenged Ian Cook he obtained no convincing excuses.

Several people then tried to speak at the same time in a somewhat unco-ordinated manner, making various suggestions in an effort to defuse the situation, but Robin Chesham was in no mood to compromise. The CE was out of his depth and could only wallow in the muddy pool around him. Robin held his fire. He had discussed exactly what he had in mind with the only colleague he could trust to keep mum and be prepared to second any motion he would propose. He had come well armed to the meeting.

He now proposed two linked motions. One, that a new shortlist be drawn up, excluding all those who had already attended the aborted Selection Committee. He then produced his copies of the CVs of all the previous applicants. Ian Cook's face blanched. Bob Randall expressed indignation at the idea, and when voting took place he abstained. The motion received a majority backing, and it was agreed that a new list be picked and candidates should attend for selection within two weeks.

There was another surprise in store for Ian Cook. Robin now contended that it was not appropriate for the Medical Director to oversee the Appointments Committee, as not only might it create a conflict of interest, but it was dispensing too much influence to the same person. Ian Cook felt affronted by this opinion, but either no one was prepared to defend him or they were all too exhausted mentally to do so. To make matters worse, Robin further proposed that the Chairman of the Appointments Committee should not be a member of the consultant staff but should be appointed from outside, preferably a lay person such as a JP or a lawyer, or from the local Health Council. He felt that a member of the hospital staff could be too easily influenced, and that a disinterested party would be far more suitable. This caused a certain amount of consternation, but in view of the very obvious scheming that had taken place no one was prepared to take an opposing view for fear of making matters worse. Robin also knew that this would make the junior staff feel less vulnerable to favouritism.

Ian Cook was shattered by this. He mumbled various expostulates, such as the whole business being like the Inquisition, but Robin hit back firmly by saying that only an autocratic fundamentalist could see in this an auto-da-fe. A vote was eventually taken and the idea accepted, perhaps more by collective guilt than by reason, but the malaise in the hospital had been so loathsome that everyone present was only too glad to see that a repetition of the previous week's gaffe had not occurred again, and clearly Robin Chesham had played on this.

As the suggestion would not only affect the Department of Surgery, it would have to be approved by the Medical Advisory Committee. On this one occasion it was universally agreed that John Gammon would act as Chairman of the temporary Selection Committee to speed matters up.

The meeting had been so contentious and had produced so many unworkable ideas that it had run out of time, and it was decided that the question of re-organisation of the junior staff would have to be postponed. This annoyed the CE, but from this baptism of fire he had realised that he had more to think about than being an administrator with a new broom. What was needed was prudent open governance, and this he would not achieve for years.

This was not a problem just at the General. Chief executives across the board were expected to put into action the precepts of so-called Thatcherism, and no one had a clear idea what it meant or was supposed to have achieved.

Soi-disant Thatcherism was largely an illusion, a concoction by a fawning media which suited its generic authorship. It never existed as far as health and welfare were concerned. It was not a philosophy and represented no evolved theories, being no more than conjectures of greed and selfishness. It did not believe in the corporate role of the State and declared society to be non-existent. Only the individual drew breath. All that mattered was his personal well-being, not the welfare of the group. We were reaching a jungle state in which only the strong had rights. Beggars and down-and-outs were littering our streets. No longer did the healthy and the wealthy take responsibility for supporting the poor and the inadequate.

Nor was Thatcherism a religion. It had no morality. It was simply doctrinaire, and as the rich and the powerful gained ascendancy, so corruption began to infiltrate the world of politics and business. The world of medicine was not exempt. One generation down the line and the omnivorous grocer's mentality would be pervading the corridors of the Palace of Westminster as it was now the streets of the Borough of Westminster with its manipulation of the sale of council houses. It could not be a science, as none of its hypotheses were ever put to the test, nor had it been subjected to any pilot studies. The long-term effects of privatising the state assets or the NHS had been given no thought. The middle classes, the working and thinking backbone of the nation, were being ripped apart and their fabric destroyed. Already that fabric was fraying at the edges. The professional classes, never distinguished for their loyalty, were becoming more and more the tools of the establishment and were making sure that the whistle blower, as a man with social principles, would be savagely ostracized.

There was certainly a malaise at every level at the General, and in this atmosphere of slow ethical decadence that had slowly crept in during the previous ten years the fact that the NHS was to be reformed created still more disaffection. It was to stop being a service to the nation and be replaced by a shopping arcade run by buyers and sellers. This, of necessity, demanded that the army of would-be executives should be almost doubled. In this climate it was not strange that events at the General were starting to wipe out devotion to the service and shatter still more any vestige of loyalty that was left. It was a worrying time for students, medical and nursing staff alike, and projecting its undermining effects ten years hence did not bear thinking about. Worst of all, a change of government was not in sight to solve this angst. No one had more severe forebodings than Robin Chesham.

* * * * * * * * *

The next day the Director of Human Resources came to see Robin. He had been asked to do so by Ian Cook, who had told him that as Medical Director he no longer wanted to be involved with appointments. Robin could not help smiling at the information. He asked if Robin would organise the short list. Robin felt that in the light of the previous day's events it would be more diplomatic to place this in the hands of an unembroiled consultant, and suggested his pairing colleague, Geoffrey Dalton.

For administrative and teamwork purposes, the Department of Surgery had organised four 'gangs' of two surgeons each, so that any one gang was on emergency duty every fourth week, while the two paired surgeons covered each other when on holiday or at conferences, which were part of their statutory study leave. The two surgeons were preferably of different age groups but with overlapping interests.

Robin had, on top of his main interest in the digestive tract, a further interest in breast disorders, which was the specialty of Geoffrey Dalton, who was younger. Between the two of them, on Dalton's appointment four years previously, they had set up a very successful breast centre with its own oncologists, pathologists and radiologist. Dalton headed it in the same way that Robin Chesham headed the gastroenterological side of the gang.

Robin therefore felt that it would be wiser for him to step down with respect to the organisation of the short list and let Dalton handle it. This was acceptable to the Director of Human Resources. He proposed to get a list ready before the end of the week and aim at the interviews on the fourth Tuesday of the month, so that by the 31st of January following, the new Senior Registrar would be in post to keep that specific rotation flowing smoothly. This met Robin's approval. He also thought it best to abstain from serving on the interviewing committee, a matter on which the Director concurred.

Later that afternoon, when Robin saw Tom, he confidentially told him of the arrangements. Tom would be rotating out of his two-year appointment with Robin in January 1992 as already planned, and as the Registrars were given a degree of choice as to where they wanted to go next, Robin advised Tom that for political reasons she should give thought to asking to work with Ian Cook. He would by then, anyway, have been fully accredited and could deputise surgically for the Medical Director. Robin's opinion was that sometimes a registrar's future could be hindered by a clash between two consultants, and what had happened the day before could come under that heading. It was politically wise - though admittedly not so good from an academic point of view - that Tom should now seek to court Ian Cook's favours. Such is politics in hospital circles that a degree of jockeying for position is often called for, and Robin above all wanted to protect Tom's future ambitions.

On the Wednesday, after his afternoon private operating session, Robin rang Georgiana from his rooms. He had called the French Horn and organised the lunch meeting for the 26th September. She was over the moon.

He had told her something of the problems at the General during their first encounter on the plane. He was now able to tell her the outcome of it all. She was to hear about a totally different side of his character, something that had hardly surfaced during their time together and was so unlike the romantic side of his personality. He opened up to her about his unease about the ethos which he felt would in time destroy his cherished NHS and make medicine a less attractive discipline, and how his colleagues looked upon him as having his own brand of centre-left views based on social justice and opposed to privilege, edacity and covert machinations. They were becoming tainted with the brush of the hired professional who was forgetting the canvas of a calling.

He had a social conscience which contrasted sharply with his current emotional conscience, of which she had become a part. Neither had yet felt a crisis of conscience, and her own emotional contrition in the ten days since they had left each other had become less and less distinct, while she could still not find an explanation for something she knew she would not be able to shake off easily. She needed to see him again, to engage anew in his physical and mental companionship, and she could not wait to do so. The 26th could not come soon enough for her.

* * * * * * * * *

The day before they were due to meet, the Selection Committee reached a unanimous verdict on the appointment of a candidate from Cardiff. Robin was thrilled. The young man in question had been the number one choice of his past short list, but he had scrupulously not mentioned it to anyone.

He was pleased for Geoffrey Dalton, as the appointee had received a first class training in breast cancerology and there was a need for an aggressive approach to the problem as the country was lagging well behind the States and the Continent in its results and little was being done about it politically or by educational bodies. Come hell or high water, he was now bent on another battle to bring about a more optimistic and robust attitude to a scourge that was still dealt with in an amateurish way by too many of his colleagues.

CHAPTER NINE

The car park stood across the road from the restaurant. Out of courtesy for his guest, Robin had arrived there earlier than the appointed rendezvous of one o'clock.

It was a sunny and warm morning for that time of early autumn. The roads from London had not been crowded and he was twenty minutes ahead of schedule. Perhaps subconsciously he wanted to be early, hoping that she too would arrive before time. He had reversed into a tucked-away parking bay, from which he would be able to observe the road and watch her arrive. He was that eager to see her.

He had taken out of his briefcase some correspondence his secretary Margaret had handed him when he left his rooms, correspondence he would usually have attended to that Wednesday morning. However, he could not concentrate. Every time a car drove by he looked up. He must have done so a dozen times before he finally saw the silver grey Celica slow down to turn into the parking area. Georgiana had already seen him, and a large smile was sweeping across her face. He smiled back. By the time she had parked he was standing by her car, and he was hugging her almost before she had got out of her seat. The ten minutes he had waited had appeared a long time, but they were now together again.

As they crossed the road he could not help holding her hand, mixing the protective with the demonstrative as he led her through a small wrought-iron gate into the French Horn. A low fire was burning in the grate in the reception area, and they decided to sit down there to study the restaurant's extensive menu while having a drink.

Robin had brought along some photographs he had received from Gustav Borg. One specially pleased him. It had been taken on the night of the Gala Dinner and showed Georgiana and himself at the main guest table engrossed in conversation. He offered it to her. He also drew her attention, in case she had not read it, to the Summit Conference on Iraq which had taken place in Finlandia Hall a couple of weeks previously.

As it was warm enough outside, they chose to have a table in the veranda section opening on to the garden and overlooking the river.

They took their time over lunch as they had so much to say and still so much to find out about each other. Robin had already asked her about her morning in Newbury. It had been a productive meeting, but they both moved away quickly from the subject of work to talk more about each other. By the time coffee was ordered they knew a good deal more.

Georgiana was an only child who had come into the world by caesarean section, as her mother's labour had failed to progress and foetal distress demanded a fairly quick intervention.

'I think my mother did not want to know about sex after that' she said jokingly. 'I certainly was given no sex education at home. It all came from a biology mistress, a spinster, at my boarding school. She knew about the physiology, but I doubt whether she knew anything about the real thing'.

Robin laughed immoderately over the last remark.

Georgiana's father was in international banking. He was at this moment in North America, and as she was not far from her parents' home she was planning to visit her mother later that afternoon. She was in no hurry to leave, knowing that her mother would not be back until after four o'clock from the high-profile recruitment agency where she worked as a character analyst on people being head-hunted for top executive posts.

As they were having coffee, Robin asked Georgiana if she had any regrets or feelings of guilt about what had happened in Helsinki. She felt she had almost squared up to it. After an initial period of inner conflict and perhaps unintentional unresponsiveness at home, she had realised that she could duplicate her emotions and cope with two non-conflicting loves, though she still needed to weigh up her emotions in terms of the continuance of a genuine and compelling relationship. They both needed time, and agreed that as they would be meeting on further occasions they could in the meantime mull over it. An intense relationship would need an intelligent, if not a rational approach, to prosper in a civilised manner.

They went for a walk to the river. In the neighbouring field several horses were grazing and as they strolled to the boundary fence, some of the animals came to greet them and followed them as they walked to the waterside.

The Thames here widens into a small lake as it bends northwards. It is a tranquil spot with overhanging willow trees shading both sides of the river. They stood on either side of a small tongue of the river, and in its waters Robin could see a full mirror image of Georgiana and the trees behind, in that darker blue that all shaded reflections have, the darker blue so typical of the paintings of Monet, to whom nature spoke always in octaves.

'I can see two of you' he said, looking into the water. 'Twice the beauty.'

'You old sop. Anyway, it works for me as well.'

From under the bridge over the road two swans appeared. They turned away from them, gliding in splendour and beauty down the limpid stream under the silent impulsion of their invisible webbed feet.

'I've seen that movement before' he said. 'I think it looked better on you.'

'You are very naughty.'

'I feel naughty' he retorted.

Georgiana sneezed. It was the fourth time he had heard this special sneeze, and he was starting to realise what it told him about how Georgiana was feeling.

'I do hope you're not allergic to me' he said.

'Actually it's the opposite. I seem to sneeze when you turn me on.'

'I wish I'd realised before. I've missed a few opportunities, then?'

'Pity we are not in a place where we can do something about it.'

'I chose this spot with higher things in mind' he said, in mock seriousness. 'Don't you think it juxtaposes just too perfectly the handiwork of man and the charm of Nature?' She laughed, and he took her hand and spun her round. 'Look at these orderly, man-made gardens.' He spun her the other way. 'Now look at the unaffected serenity of the river. I nurture the wish, when the time comes, of having my ashes scattered here. It is just so peaceful.'

He stood silent for a moment, and she was not sure how to respond.

'You can see why in Childe Harold Byron said 'I love not man less but Nature more' Robin went on.

'It certainly is a lovely spot. I think young Byron was on to something.'

They both paused for a moment.

'You obviously like his poetry' she said. 'Do you think he has been unfairly maligned?'

'Are you referring to his attachment to his half-sister or to the stark realism of his general philosophy and his condemnation of hypocrisy in English Society?'

'I was thinking of the sister. That supposed admission of incest which was used indirectly to drive him out of the country.'

Robin found this an interesting question and they sat down on a low wall to discuss it. He felt the word 'incest' was used too loosely and too frequently by social workers, the police and the law. Not enough thought, he felt, was given to gene-related attraction. This puzzled Georgiana, who wanted clarification. Robin expounded his thoughts.

If in a pure family situation a physical relationship developed between members who had lived together since birth, be it a parent-child or brother-sister one, then clearly the word 'incest' applied and it would be deemed unhealthy. If the members had been separated at birth or sometime after and had not met until well into adulthood, and therefore had no previous environmental or emotional ties, it is more likely that genetic traits in common could trigger a mutual sexual attraction. Furthermore, sensory memories of the other person, be they tactile, auditory or olfactory, could easily awaken emotions of intimacy. It would be wrong in such circumstances to criminalise the act.

'How does this affect Byron?' she interjected.

'Well, he's a typical example of incest that wasn't incest' said Robin. He went on to explain it.

Augusta, Byron's half sister by his father's first marriage, had been an infant when her mother died and was fostered by her maternal grandmother. Byron was born four years later, the only child of his father's second marriage, and had little knowledge of her. Augusta was some twenty years old when Byron first corresponded with her and they did not meet until some time later. A physical relationship may have begun by the time Augusta had become a lady-in-waiting to Queen Charlotte. She was beautiful, and shared Byron's laughter, complexion and self-consciousness.

Augusta by then had a daughter - 'Your namesake, Georgiana!' remarked Robin - by her marriage to her first cousin, George Leigh. She was with Byron in London in August 1813, by which time they could have become lovers. Her second daughter, Medora, was born in April 1814, a date which was held as highly suggestive of that daughter being Byron's, but it did not preclude George's paternity. What is interesting is that it is held, without good evidence, that of all Augusta's children, Byron was fondest of Medora.

Still more interesting is that Augusta, George Leigh and Byron were all grandchildren of the same female lineage, that of Sophia Trevanion, who, to compound the situation, married her first cousin, John Byron. There was thus, over three successive generations, an intermixing of common chromosomes, a real cauldron of familial genes.

Sophia was an intelligent, highly intellectual and beautiful woman who enjoyed the company of Dr Johnson. No doubt some of her genes were passed on to both Augusta and Byron. It is understandable that in a poem to his 'own sweet sister' he would end it by saying:

'We are entwined: let death come slow or fast,
The tie which bound the first endures the last'.

'But it did not stop there' said Robin. 'Georgiana ended up marrying her cousin, Henry Trevanion. And then, to make matters worse, Henry fell obsessively in love with Medora and seduced her.'

'Phew!' responded Georgiana.

'Well, you can see what I mean by incest not being necessarily an act within a family set-up but one that could be confused with an attraction between genes of separate but related families. We shouldn't look upon Byron's affair with his half-sister as so heinous when we take into account the time factor. There are other historical examples, as well as fictional ones. Wagner in The Valkyr has Siegmund and Sieglinde fall in love at first sight, only to realise that they are brother and sister separated from each other at birth.

Nonetheless they indulge in a carnal relationship, out of which is born Siegfried.

'I believe that as we study genetics more and more, we may well find that there are specific genes - genes of love, maybe - that bring together people carrying them regardless of their sexuality. The difference between the two types deserves studying. The French have a saying: 'chasser le naturel, il revient au gallop'. '

'What's bred in the bone will come out in the flesh.'

'Exactly.'

Robin explained that with the increasing fashion for sperm donation, to be followed by egg donation and probably, in years to come, the exchange of genetic material between cells, the incidence of unrecognised genetic incest was bound to increase. It would surely trigger off a review of the ethics of reproduction and sexual relationships. By the end of the decade man's genomic profile would have been mapped and Nature's hold on the secrets of paternity, maternity and intersexuality would have been laid bare to law and society.

'Shouldn't there be a register of donors?' suggested Georgiana.

'Yes. There is pressure to have one so that in the future someone procreated by donation could avoid accidentally marrying a half-brother or a half-sister. It won't solve the problem completely, though. Many children are born out of wedlock. But it will at least reduce the risk of such marriages.'

He explained that our genes are in essence molecular computers which an evolutionary past has programmed to determine our future. We are bequeathed at birth a book of inherited memories or instincts, each chapter with its own confidential code. Anyone who is the bearer of a matching code can key into our secrets and invade our innermost selves and our most guarded privacy. That invasion all too frequently creates a powerful bond and a desire for carnal intimacy. The female animal seeks in the act her necessary quest for the best available genes, and thus a better outcome for her progeny. To the human male, recreation has overtaken reproduction, and its repetitiveness makes him more territorial than procreative, allowing reason to be displaced by the worst of emotions: jealousy, which in a world of circumspect feminism is better handled by the more intelligent females of the species.

What is love? What makes one love? What is the predestination that draws two people together? Is an inherited lodestone the begetter of the acquired one?

They went back to the car park and sat in Robin's car. 'I want you to listen to one of my tapes' he said, switching on the cassette player. It was Lara's Theme from Dr Zhivago.

Georgiana leaned over to him and rested her head on his left shoulder.

'Give me a kiss' she said. 'I've missed you so much.'

Robin obliged. They could not be seen from the road. They hugged each other until the music died, both recalling the time when it had been the background to their first passionate encounter. It had become their song.

Georgiana looked at him and sneezed. He bent over and kissed her forehead.

'I think it's time you got going' he said.

'When am I going to see you again?'

'I suppose in Paris, at Didier's Journées in November.'

'Can't we meet again next month? I have to be around here on Thursday the 25th of October.'

'Greedy! Might be possible.'

'I'll have to come to Heathrow on the 25th to pick Philip up – he's back from the Far East around six in the morning. My parents will be away, but I can stay at their place for convenience. Couldn't we meet on the 24th?'

Robin looked at his diary. Margaret would be away on holiday that week and he had decided not to make any appointments at his rooms. Instead he was planning a morning in the medical library before going to the Royal Academy for a Monet exhibition. His wife had been to see it the week before and had waxed lyrical about it.

Georgiana's eyes opened wide. It was too good an opportunity to miss.

'Can I come too? Please!'

She was still due several days of her annual leave, so she could easily take the Wednesday off. She would drive to her parents' home the night before, dump her car there, take the coach to Victoria Station and join him that afternoon at the RA. Perhaps he could run her back to Henley, she suggested with a twinkle in her eyes. She still had her own room at her parents' place.

Robin laughed at her ingenuity. He knew what she was after, and he was certainly game. It would be a lovely afternoon, and neither would be playing truant. They could hardly contain their excitement at the thought of another tryst less than a month away.

On her way to her mother's, Georgiana thought about the gene business. If there were such a thing as a gene of love, had their sudden mutual attraction been a quirk of nature - a chance meeting of two similar genes? Had Robin found in her enquiry about Byron an opportunity to raise an uncharted side of human nature? She felt it was unintentional and had not been engineered. Did it give her now an opportunity to talk herself out of any possible guilt feelings? She was not sure, but at least it was a plausible explanation. She pondered over it without interruption, and by the time she reached the house where so much of her childhood and young adult life had been spent she thought she had begun to understand herself - and for that matter, her mother – rather better. She had inadvertently woken up to a new way of looking at her own emotional needs and the sudden carnal yearning that had overtaken her after so many years of normal and still stable domestic life.

The most important outcome of their hours together in Sonning had been that their previous physical relationship had emerged as more than a senseless and impulsive infatuation. They were both quite certain now that something deeper than an impetuous, superficial urge had drawn them together. Something else was at play - but what? Would they have to organise themselves in such a way that those they cherished most would not be deprived of their love and loyalty and would still remain dear to them?

They both realised fully what they were undertaking and how they should henceforth marshal their emotions. Had their Sonning meeting now sealed their fate?

CHAPTER TEN

In spite of the disquiet at the General with respect to the so-called reformation of the NHS, Geoffrey Dalton continued to improve the service of the Breast Unit. However he was constantly having to face the administrative hindrance of poor-quality managers.

One particular case had caused him much vexation. A patient called Rachel Hudson had been given an urgent appointment to see him at the open-access clinic, having found a lump in her right breast.

In view of Rachel's age and of the fact that her mother had died when Rachel had been only 21, Dalton went into her background in some depth. She was forty-eight. She used the surname of her common-law husband, with whom she had lived since her late teens, having fallen out with her father. She had two children, both in their twenties. Biopsies had revealed the lesion to be an aggressive one with genetic overtones.

At Dalton's request, Rachel had come back a few days later with as much historical detail as she could obtain from other members of the family. She had brought a cutting announcing her birth. It read: 'Cope - 18th January 1942. To Rose and Jake, a daughter Rachel'.

The notice had been in the birthday column of the local paper in Golders Green. Jake Cope had been born Jacob Kopelsky. He was of Jewish descent from White Russia, the family having settled for a while in Poland and then moved to Germany, where they had run a small tailor's shop on the outskirts of Leipzig. With the rumblings of war and the aggression of the Nazi régime towards anything remotely Jewish, Jacob's father advised his only son to leave Germany. He had a distant acquaintance in London's East End, also a tailor, and there the young man was eventually offered asylum. He had no trade of his own, nor the ability to undertake office work. With the little money he had managed to take out with him, his host advised him to buy a second-hand taxi and earn his living that way. A hard worker and no clock watcher, he had made a reasonable success of it.

Through the shop he had met Rose, a seamstress and a local girl, and their romance blossomed. Her father had been an infantryman in the First World War; he had returned home after the war, married soon after, and Rose was born in late 1919. In 1939 she married Jacob Kopelsky, who by then had been advised to anglicise his name and become Jake Cope.

They moved to Golders Green, fearing the bombing of the East End, and lived in a small flat above a shop at the bottom end of North End Road. This had suited Rose, as the hospital up the hill needed a pair of hands in their linen room, and Rose was ideally suited for that job. She was soon pregnant, but unluckily lost the baby. It was not until two years later that Rachel was born. She remained the only child, as Rose lost her next baby from jaundice soon after birth and never became pregnant again.

Rachel grew up in Golders Green and went to the local school, but never really made friends there. Her roots seemed to be with her aunts and uncles in the East End, while her father's philosophy of life, very much Eastern European, found no echo in the way young people wanted to live in the late fifties and early sixties. The clashes at home were so frequent that Rachel would often go and stay with her cousins, especially at week-ends. There she met Tony Hudson, who was several years her senior, and moved in with him.

She found employment locally and was clearly enlightened enough not to have children endlessly, being among the earliest of her generation to take advantage of the advent of the contraceptive pill in 1962. They were a close couple and were responsible enough to plan their two children, though they never saw the need to get married. They both worked, had a good joint income and had moved up socially and economically.

Rachel saw her mother only occasionally, and with her inability to relate fully to her father, child and parents grew apart. This was unfortunate, as Jake prospered, and by the early fifties had a fleet of taxis. She had not been aware of any health problems of her mother's until late 1962, when one of her aunts told her that her mother had been diagnosed with advanced breast cancer. Rose had continued to work at the local hospital until quite late in her illness, and died on 18th January 1963, the same day as the Leader of the Opposition, Hugh Gaitskell, and in the same hospital. It also happened to be Rachel's twenty-first birthday. A further coincidence was that Mrs Gaitskell, like Rachel's father, was of Russian Jewish origin. Rachel could not forget any of these historical events.

Geoffrey Dalton wanted to find out more. 'Any way of finding out from other members of your family what your grandmother died of?' he asked.

Rachel had established that her grandmother had died in one of the local hospitals from what had been thought to be lung cancer. She was not yet fifty at the time and had never smoked. Her admission could only have been at the General or at the North Poplar, as they were the only hospitals serving that district.

Geoffrey delved into the defunct notes of the North Poplar, where he found that though the diagnosis had been of a right lung lesion with a secondary involvement of the brain, the most likely diagnosis was a breast primary, the more so that women in those days rarely smoked. There was thus a very strong possibility of a genetic background to the cancer which had plagued three generations. Luckily, Rachel's two children were boys.

Both Rose and her mother came from a poor background, with no health ethos, and would have sought medical advice too late. The poorer and the more deprived a family, the greater the toll of cancer, a state of affairs that Geoffrey Dalton often pointed out to his students and juniors. Rachel, more educated and of a higher income group, had come to him early enough to be treated in good time and improve her chances of longer survival.

The Breast Unit was a very efficient one, and within days all investigations on Rachel had been completed. They showed no detectable spread, though microscopic lesions could never be excluded. The oncologist, the pathologist and the surgeons (Robin always joined them for decision making) met shortly after and agreed that chemotherapy should precede surgery. Rachel was to be started on a very novel treatment regimen which, though not of long standing, made sense and was logical. Results from the States and the Continent were already promising. She would have to go on an ambulatory twenty-four hour instillation of an anti-cancer drug and the progress of the treatment would be regularly and carefully monitored. It was all explained to her and her husband and the risks involved fully discussed. With her tragic family history, the gloves had to be off. Husband and wife understood this clearly. She was fully counselled about what to expect, and every psychological support was offered.

The Breast Clinic possessed only two mini-pumps for such treatments. One would not become available for several weeks, while the other would remain in use for at least four months. It was clear that more pumps would be needed. They were costly - over a thousand pounds apiece - and could be temperamental, and if either of the two in use broke down, the ongoing treatment would be in jeopardy.

Robin and Geoffrey made an urgent request to the Director of

Supplies for two pumps, but as the sum involved exceeded £1000, it had to be referred to the Supplies Committee. Bureaucracy was in full force. Non-professional directors could neither know in which direction to go nor take responsibility for their actions, and did not have the judgment to take decisions. They were lay administrators who had to hide behind a faceless committee. This was part of free market forces. One might as well have been in a souk in Casablanca. Everything had to be bargained for - jobs, beds, parking spaces, lives.

At the ensuing Supplies Committee meeting, Robin supported Geoffrey and a battle began. There were insufficient funds to provide the modest £2000 required for a life-and-death facility. The Supplies Director had a waiting list for funds on a first-come-first-served basis, not on clinical priority. Ian Cook had applied for £75,000 to set up a project for the removal of gallbladders by the new technique of laparoscopic ('keyhole') surgery. It was still in its infancy, and apart from in a few places, such as Dundee, few had any experience of the method. Those who had set up such projects were often pioneering them without previous training and many unfortunate, if not fatal, results were being reported.

'Who'll do the work?' Robin enquired.

'I've arranged for my registrar to visit a colleague in the Midlands and watch the operation being performed' said Cook.

'I don't think that's good enough' said Robin. 'It's like asking someone to drive a car after having been a passenger. It would need proper training over a couple of months or so in a dedicated unit to achieve meaningful competence.'

Geoffrey Dalton took up the cudgels on behalf of his patients in need of life-saving pumps.

'No one dies of a gall bladder problem when they're treated by the classical operation, though laparoscopic surgery may be more elegant and easier to bear.' He said. 'This new method is not likely to save lives. It probably won't save money either. It will almost certainly result in fatalities during the learning curve of the surgeon. On the other hand, my patients will suffer or die from their cancer for lack of the necessary equipment.'

It was stalemate, as is so often the case in such disputes. To place the onus on the medical profession when the problem lies with a government obsessed with a free market and untested ideas borders on immorality. The Director of Supplies felt that the matter would have to be referred to the Chief Executive as arbiter - an arbiter who did not understand the nuances of medicine, held patients as mere customers in the supermarket of treatment, and believed that money saving and performance bonuses for himself must come before patients. Certainly he would not have the judgment to take meaningful decisions. But this was 1990, and Thatcherism was rife.

The theory was that if laparoscopic surgery brought in more patients and treatment became cheaper, market forces would apply. Demand seemed more important than need. No study had shown as yet that this method was cheaper. Dogma prevailed rather than common sense or compassion. The CE vetoed the request for the pumps, and favoured, in support of his Medical Director, the spending of £75,000. That sum was available, yet £2000 for the pumps was not. Such was the madness of the free market.

Worse still was that false saving was more important than life. It was an age of feral politics, not clinical common sense.

Geoffrey Dalton had to explain to Rachel and her husband the quandary the Unit was in and that pumps could be temperamental.

'We do not have a free pump. If Rachel's pump failed during treatment, there would not be a back-up one either. We are trying to get some help from various charities associated with the Unit, but no luck so far.'

A few days later Rachel called his secretary at the hospital with some good news. Her father had heard of her illness and had come to see her. She had explained what was happening, and Jake had offered to pay for a pump to cover his daughter's treatment. Geoffrey invited Jake and Rachel to the Unit to meet the team, and he brought with him a cheque for £1500. The pump was ordered straight away and a small reception was organised for Jake to officially hand over the 'Jake pump', as it would be known.

Despite their long estrangement, paternal love was still there. Rachel's illness had brought father and daughter together. Some good had come out of the administrative machinations of the hospital.

CHAPTER ELEVEN

It was the last week of October, and autumn was still masquerading as summer. The build-up of armed forces in the Middle East was going on relentlessly in an effort to bring Saddam Hussein to his senses and stop his brutal raping of Kuwait. The Helsinki Summit Conference on the 9th September had demonstrated a significant display of unity among all powers present, and both Bush and Gorbachev, representing the two superpowers, had showed unusual accord in opposing Iraq's violation of Kuwait's territory.

Russia was still in ferment and Gorbachev was wooing the West. In Trans- Caucasus, Islamic fundamentalists were causing unrest. They were joined by what Gorbachev called the 'rabble' in denouncing his perestroika, the restructuring of Russia's economic, political and social climate. The sea-change that had taken place in Russia had hardly been appreciated in the West. Few had realised the impact of Gorbachev's rethinking of Russia's political principles in persuading the Communist Party of the Soviet Union (CPSU) to relinquish its eighty years of monopoly of power and move the country into a freer society, allowing the creation of a multi-party system, and a degree of devolution.

In early February, that year, the CPSU had backed these reforms and in March Gorbachev had been made President of the USSR and Communist Party General Secretary. Saddam Hussein might not have appreciated the full implication of this, as well as the rapprochement between the Soviet Union and the West, for on the 17th October he warned the USSR that if Moscow gave to the US classified information about Russian weapons sold to Iraq, the departure of Soviet nationals would be jeopardised. He had more than 5000 Soviets working in Iraq, both in the oil industry and the rearmament programme of Baghdad. Perhaps he was relying on the unrest in the Union, more so from a certain Boris Yeltsin, who had become a power in the land. It would not be past Hussein to exploit any discord between the President of the USSR and this new political star in Russia.

Byelorussia and Ukraine had amalgamated into the Russian Federation, which encompassed almost two-thirds of the USSR's population. In March Yeltsin had won a seat in the Russian Supreme Soviet, and he had become the first president of this powerful Russian Federation. He was, next to Gorbachev, the most influential man in Russia, if not the most dangerous.

Robin called Georgiana that week, and they discussed the events going on in Russia.

'Gorbachev has won the approval of the Supreme Soviet of his reforms by 333 votes to 12' Robin commented. 'It's a massive endorsement of his economic policies.'

'I agree. However, this man Yeltsin says they're not radical enough and not swift enough. It looks like a clear challenge to the new leadership.'

Robin, still concerned about what was going on in Iraq, said he was certain that Hussein would be watching this as carefully as he was the economic unrest in the USA.

'He's going to be looking at the so-called 'special relationship' between us and the States, with Bush seeking to shift more towards Germany, it seems' added Georgiana.

Three weeks previously, Germany had undergone reunification. This had received the full support of Gorbachev. He had agreed with Kohl that the destiny of the Germans was a matter for them and no one else. France, however, was fearing a return to German hegemony in Europe and was pressing still more for a unified Continent as a way of buffering German domination.

'We may well hear more about this next month' Robin said, knowing Didier was not very enamoured of the States. 'Bush is hyping up the American public with noises that Saddam's war machine needs to be destroyed to assure peace in the Middle East.'

'And protect the oil reserves of the world.'

This, no doubt, would have some impact on the declining American economy, to which was now grafted the problem of the American hostages held by Saddam. Georgiana thought it was laughable that Jesse Jackson, on a trip of self-indulgence for a syndicated television group, had managed to bring back a dozen or so women and children and a few sick men. This was receiving some degree of criticism by the news media and indirectly by Bush.

'I'm not sure I go along with Douglas Hurd' Robin added. 'He seems to think battles are still won on the playing fields of Eton. This is almost reverting to the pre-World War 1 order of a traditional 'concert of nations', whereby just a few great powers should determine the fate of the world and run it.'

'I tend to agree. The latest news is that the Desert Rats are being moved from their posting in Germany to Saudi Arabia. They'll be under US command. This means committing ground forces to the war zone.'

'Yes' replied Robin. 'It's not going to please our generals. It's just going to fuel more unrest in this country.'

The 'Stop the War' campaign was rambling on to no clear purpose. The Europhobic Tories were in as much disarray as ever, not only over the Iraq Supergun affair but above all over Europe. Meanwhile the Prime Minister was getting ready with her Foreign Secretary to attend the Versailles Conference on Security and Co-operation in Europe - the CSCE - a month hence.

'We're going to be in Paris then' Georgiana said-.

'You're right. The papers to-day were saying that Mitterand was dispatching a French force to the Middle East. What's laughable is that the deposed Willi Brandt is seeking a private visit to Hussein on humanitarian grounds, having raised money from German companies to buy medicine and food for the Iraqis. I can't see this visit being blessed by Kohl.'

'He has enough on his hands with the re-unification of Germany,' she interrupted him, 'not to mention what's going on in Israel with elected governments collapsing one after the other. Saddam must have realised that Israel would not be able to interfere with his annexing of Kuwait.'

To this external world of turmoil and confusion in the first year of the last decade of the century was added the malaise of the ill-thought-out reforms at the General. They were adding greatly to the mental anguish of the workforce there. It was also unclear what would be expected of the hospital in the event of having to cope with the injured from a Middle East conflict. No plans had been mapped out to that effect and, as usual, crisis management would be the order of the day. It was an appalling situation, without direction from a weary and ungifted government. Any sensitive person could not help feeling disturbed at what was going on. To Robin, the thought of seeing Georgiana at the Monet exhibition within forty-eight hours helped to calm the turbulence, both in the hospital and in the world beyond.

CHAPTER TWELVE

Cio-Cio was in Louise's bad books. She had that morning behaved totally out of character and was now in deep disgrace. She had an internal clock which would wake her about eleven most mornings, or she would, through her acute sense of hearing, pick up the distant sound of the school bell giving the under eights a break. She would then quickly make her way to the school, some three houses away, to play with the children. She was everyone's friend. They knew her name and her home telephone number from the small disc on her pink collar.

Cio-Cio's favourite game was hopscotch. She would sit by the rough rectangle drawn on the concrete of the playground and wait until the children started hopping. Then she would promote or hinder the progress of the flat stone, to the amusement of children and teachers alike. She knew she was being entertaining and had her own sense of feline vanity.

For a seventeen-year-old cat she was in many ways kittenish. This made her delightfully attractive to the children. As is so often the case, she had been acquired by Louise and Robin because their two children wanted a pet, but the parents had ended up looking after her once the children had lost interest.

Once the bell had rung again to summon the children to their classes, Cio-Cio would quietly go back home having enjoyed herself. That morning, for some unexplained reason, she followed a group of the children back to their classroom. There, she insisted in jumping from one desk to another as if looking for something purposefully hidden from her. She became such a nuisance that the teacher chucked her out of the classroom and shut her out, but within minutes, she had come in again through an open window and was distracting the children once more.

Again she was ejected and the window closed, but Cio-Cio was not prepared to be defeated and made her way back through an open fanlight. The annoyed teacher then rang the number on her collar and asked Louise to collect the cat. Cio-Cio miaowed her protest all the way back, but she was quickly confined to the house and the cat-flap door latched.

Somehow she managed to escape. She went back to the same classroom and once more, to her great embarrassment, Louise had to go and fetch her.

The tone of Louise's voice told Cio-Cio she had blotted her copybook. This time she stayed quietly on the left arm of her mistress, though without the purr of contentment she usually emitted when she was carried. She knew she was in trouble. She was then firmly locked in a bathroom until school was over.

All this had made Louise late in preparing a small tea party for Tom's wife, Geraldine, and their two small children. Hopefully Cio-Cio would still be in the mood to play with them.

Geraldine was a bright girl and a perfect match for Tom. She had become a Paediatric Registrar at the Royal Archway some six months previously. It was an ideal appointment as they lived in Highgate, minutes away from the hospital. Geraldine could be on call from home on her duty nights. She had found a girl childminder prepared to live in. On Tuesdays, which were Geraldine's half-days off, the girl attended her day classes and had the evening off. Geraldine would collect the children that afternoon from their nursery school and was thus able to join Louise on this occasion.

The children could not quite yet say Sylvia, so they called the minder Via. An eighteen-year-old adopted daughter of one of Robin's patients, she was of limited intelligence, but she was affectionate and loved children. She had gone through the usual training demanded of future minders and her parents were delighted that she would be taken into a professional home. The children had quickly accepted her, and Tom and Geraldine were very pleased with her. She was a homely person, and on her free evenings or weekends would often go to visit her parents in Kew. Twice a week she went to day classes while the children were at school. The routine was for Geraldine to drop them at the nursery school, almost opposite the hospital, while the minder would collect them in the early afternoon. The proximity of school and hospital was such that Geraldine could be there within five minutes if necessary. It was a happy and convenient set-up.

To Louise and Robin, the juniors of his surgical team were treated as their extended family. Quite frequently, Tom and Geraldine would join them for tea on a Sunday, or occasionally Geraldine and the children would be invited for tea on a Tuesday, as on this day, Louise being very fond of her.

Geraldine was of Anglo-Irish descent. She had had a very strict upbringing by a catholic mother, from whom she had inherited deep blue eyes and dark hair. Throughout her university years in London Geraldine had lived at home in a very protected ambience, rarely exposed to alcohol. She had met Tom during her first year as a house officer and he had soon realised how susceptible to drinks she was, even wine. She therefore never drank while on duty or on emergency call.

Tom and Geraldine were deeply in love with each other, something that Robin and Louise had realised from early on. It was reflected in the names of their children. Geraldine had wanted her first son to be named after his father so, he was called Thomas.

When the second child was born - a girl - Tom chose Geraldine's second name, Cora, very much an Irish one, for his daughter. The children were just over a year apart and Thomas was very protective of his little sister at school.

They loved visiting the house in St John's Wood, especially to see Cio-Cio. Louise had therefore gone upstairs before their arrival to let the cat out. At any other time Cio-Cio would have got up immediately and joined Louise, but she was still assailed by her sense of guilt and stayed put. She felt chastisement profoundly and it was usually only at night, when Louise and Robin retired, that she would come into bed and be friendly, as if to seek forgiveness before the day was over.

Thomas wore his favourite T-shirt, which bore a large picture of Thomas the Tank Engine.

'That's my name' he said to Louise, pointing to the lettering.

'There isn't a train named after me' interrupted Cora. 'It's not fair.'

'You'll need to write a story about an aeroplane and call it Cora' said Louise to pacify her.

Cio-Cio heard the children's voices and was down like a shot.

'Can I pick her up?' shouted Cora. And without waiting to be permitted to do so, she established full possession of the cat, provoking protests from her brother.

The house was Georgian in style. The front porch carried Grecian columns, dividing the façade into well balanced symmetrical halves carrying on the ground floor two windows on either side, corresponding respectively to a substantial drawing room and a long dining one.

Geraldine loved the elegance of the drawing room, more so the large painting over the mantelpiece, the work of Louise, who was no mean artist. She had had two 'one-man' exhibitions in London, and a gallery off New Cavendish Street hung her paintings. Robin was very proud of her talent. Many years before, when they had moved into their present house, he had added a large Victorian summer room to the back of the house. It spanned almost the whole width of the house at the rear, opening into a morning room at the back of the drawing room on the right. On the left it opened into the kitchen behind the dining room. He wanted it to be a studio for her work with all the advantages of daylight for painting. Her easel stood in one corner, while on the other a double door opened on to a rose garden, which was overlooked by Robin's own study, adjacent to the summer room.

Louise had prepared the tea in the summer room so that the children could roam in and out into the back garden as they wished. Two old swings from earlier days which still hung from a tree were soon commandeered by Thomas and Cora. Cio-Cio, abandoned to her great indignation by the children, joined the adults.

They all had an enjoyable afternoon together, the more so since Louise had not seen Geraldine on her own for quite a while. She was very impressed on how well focused Geraldine was and how much more worldly wise and knowledgeable her generation was. Above all, Geraldine had understood how a system obsessed with pure career orientation could flounder if young doctors became disillusioned with their work - more so women, who were now becoming the majority at student level.

'I am working hard at my membership' she said. 'There's no chance of getting a higher post without it. But I know it's far more important for me to be good at my job and achieve a high level of competence clinically than to try and move into academic research.'

'I think Robin would agree with you there. He feels that too often juniors are pushed into producing academic papers of poor value just to collect a dubious portfolio. It's doubtful whether so-called research improves clinical ability. It also means spending a couple of years or more on a futile project. Unfortunately there is a compulsion to produce as many doctorates as possible, just for the aggrandisement of academic units.'

Geraldine concurred. She was keener on pursuing a good clinical programme that would lead her to a useful permanent job, but was aware of the pressure to publish.

At supper that evening, Louise told Robin how much she had savoured the couple of hours she had spent with Geraldine and talked about the latter's views on her career.

'I'll like to see both of them reach the top' Robin remarked. 'Tom is destined for a distinguished career. With a couple of retirements in a year or two, he could well land a post at the General. The problem for Geraldine would be finding a senior registrar post and then a consultant's appointment within the same ten miles radius. It could be quite a hard job for her.'

He thought that at some stage, having invited them one Sunday, he would advise Geraldine to look at the retirement profile in paediatrics within the North London catchment area, as she would need to start planning at an early stage. Events were moving so quickly and so haphazardly in the NHS that the system could easily crack up. It would never be too early to study future possibilities. Furthermore, the legal profession was exploiting any blame in treatment to further a claim, usually a spurious one. It was essential for their bank balance. Such specious litigation was demanding more and more that consultants prove their expertise before undertaking unusual commitments. Liability and negligence were becoming more and more confused and were proving a goldmine for the legal profession, more so those exploiting free legal aid about improbable clinical inadvertence.

After supper, over a cup of coffee, Robin talked to Louise about yet another change at the General. He had been, for a couple of years, one of the 'Three Wise Men' at the hospital. This was a trio of consultants chosen for their objectivity and even-handedness to deal with any serious complaints made about members of the clinical staff. With the changes in the administrative structure of the hospital, the Medical Director and the Chief Executive were demanding a place on this confidential committee.

Robin was unhappy about this. It was bringing into a purely professional enquiry an administrative judicial consideration that could remove from office a medical person before all the facts had been established. You would be guilty until proved innocent. This could easily wreck someone's career while you were waiting for culpability to be proved, or more likely not proved. He was concerned about this and he was inclined to resign from that committee.

He was now soliciting Louise's counsel, as he placed much reliance on her balanced understanding of politics. She was good in this field. While she was still in her teens, her father had been a junior minister in a previous government. She had often been a bystander during political discussions in which strategy and tactics were often worked out, and it had brushed off on her. She could prognosticate the moves of administrators with the precision of a chess player.

'Resigning would betray the trust of the colleagues who elected you' she said. 'They need your sense of detachment. Agree to let the two executives to be present at your meetings without judgment being imposed by them. Instead, once the three of you have come to a conclusion, give them the responsibility of implementing your decision. If they choose to act against your joint advice, place still more responsibility on their shoulders. That would emasculate them.'

Robin had to smile at her perspicacity. He agreed to delay any resignation on his part until he had proposed the stratagem to his two colleagues. They were to meet the following week to interview two members of the medical staff who had been reported to the Medical Director. He never mentioned such specific problems to Louise, as he felt they were confidential hospital matters, but they were very much in his thoughts.

One of the doctors, a house officer who lived in the residential quarters of the hospital, was alleged to have been taking drugs. He had been reported by a cleaner who said she had found a syringe and a sheathed used needle under his bed. She had also stated that she had more than once seen a male friend leave his room early in the morning. To the Presbyterian Medical Director, this smacked of homosexuality linked to drug taking, more so that analysis of the trace contents of the syringe had revealed the presence of the potent analgesic Pethidine.

The other person reported to the Director was one of the thoracic surgeons, Ronald Muller. This came from the Nurse Manager of one of his wards. She felt that too many of his patients had died within days of their operations, She had kept tabs on this over the past year. There had apparently been a recent disagreement between the two of them and malice on the part of the Nurse Manager was suspected. If her complaint proved to be justified, this was likely to bring about the possibility of professional misconduct, and could be very serious. It could not be swept under the carpet, particularly as Ronald Muller was a close friend of Ian Cook.

Robin wondered whether Cook had by now tipped off Muller and prepared him for an enquiry into his clinical results. Where does friendship stop and administrative duty start when colleagues are involved? There was no clear answer to this when a medical person has administrative duties. This was part of Robin's malaise.

That night when they went to bed, they found Cio-Cio stretched across the middle of their bed with her head at the level of their pillows. She was there to seek their pardon in her usual way for her bad behaviour earlier that day. It was also her way of showing that she bore Louise no grudge. She was not prepared to be moved.

'She makes a pretty effective contraceptive' said Louise.

'We'll see about that' countered Robin.

CHAPTER THIRTEEN

The 23rd of October proved a very busy day at work for Georgiana. She had to deal in advance with various tasks which she would have planned for the day of her return from Heathrow. By the time she had left her office it was gone seven o'clock, so she decided not to drive to Henley that night. She would leave early the next morning instead. She could get there in good time, settle down and leave her car.

The next morning she took a coach from Henley to Reading in time to catch the 12.30 to Paddington. She arrived at the RA just before half past one. Robin was in the courtyard waiting for her, a radiant smile on his face.

He suggested they each use the audio cassette commentary, as this was the best guide to the exhibition. It was a beautifully-spoken narration about the collection, dealing particularly well with the way he had painted the haystacks under every kind of light, as he had done with the long row of poplars lining the river which flowed past his home in Giverny. Rouen cathedral, the Thames, the rocks at Entretat - all were shown in shade, mist or sun. It was a study in eternity.

Before the Impressionistes, France had no school of painting of its own. Art was still steeped in the classicism started by Poussin in the 17th century and championed by David and Ingres in the two centuries that followed. Japanese prints arrived in Paris in the middle of the last century and brought a new dimension to painting. Painters, however, went on painting what their eyes saw, though Manet had created a new technique that gave the impression of movement by superimposing dark areas over his light vistas before the paler pigments had been given time to dry. Painting was moving, for the first time, from the visible to the perceived. The moods of a day were being translated into emotions. It was left to Monet to take this a step further.

As a child in Le Havre among the fishing boats at the mouth of the Seine, Monet was fascinated by the reflections in the water of the houses, trees and boats. As the wind rustled the water, these reflections would have created, in his subconscious, the constant changing appearances of light and shade on the disturbed surface of the river. Later in life this led him to render what he felt on canvas. There would be forever a juxtaposition of strong pigments narrating the changing hues in a scenery as the sun played through the notes of the spectrum. He painted light alongside shade, making the latter nothing more than a form of darkness made visible. Then to add to the picture of his poplars, in various light incidences or bent by the wind, he would bring to life the seasons in the way he had depicted his haystacks. A morning effect would be compared to one during an overcast hour, or at the end of the day. The encrusted surfaces of the stacks in summer would contrast with the effects of frost or snow in winter. He would paint Waterloo Bridge lost in fog or evanescent in a dying sun. All this was to be seen in a brilliant collection of paintings brought together by the Royal Academy. They had never been seen like this before.

Standing in front of these paintings, they were nothing more nor less than two onlookers in a daily crowd of thousands, lost in their personal dreams, aware of each other's silent presence, yet subjugated by the genius of the man who could make a tranquil lake speak of its desire for a water lily as a Japanese bridge would of its love for a curve. Who, in the circumstances, would not have felt the inner elation of togetherness or intimacy? They had shared this pleasure, and in sharing it they had doubled it. There was no monotony in their acknowledged monogamy. Both were happy with their respective partners. They had plunged into a torrid relationship, yet they wanted from each other more than just the physical. Some powerful force was driving them into each other's arms, propelling them into a state of happiness that they could not explain.

They stayed for an hour and a half, slowly making their way through each room, stopping every now and then to be together again and exchange their appreciation of a man who had changed the classical concept of painting and had moved away from the pre-occupation with actuality to a study of the subjectivity of forms. Robin's analysis of the paintings cast a new light on her understanding of Monet, and she was finding yet another facet of his personality.

The artist had projected on to their retinas not just light and shade but sensations. Their bonding had awakened in them a profound sharing of similar sensations, heightening still more their desire for each other.

'Would you like tea before we leave?' said Robin.

Georgiana had eaten on the train and declined the offer. Yet she was longing to be alone with him.

'How much time can you spare me?' she asked.

'I'm in no hurry' he replied. 'My wife is attending an Arts Society meeting all day and she's not likely to be home before eight. My whole afternoon is yours.'

'Can we go to Henley before the afternoon traffic builds up?'

'Why not?'

They found it impossible to hail a taxi. Robin had left his car at his rooms in Devonshire Place.

'Let's walk it' said Georgiana. 'It's only a few minutes away.'

They went up Old Bond Street and from there up New Bond Street to Welbeck Street before turning into Weymouth Street. On their way they stopped a few times to look at the many attractive shops. A picture gallery caught Georgiana's eyes and she stopped to look at some paintings in the window.

'These are good' she said. Robin smiled.

'What's so funny?'

'They're Louise's, my wife. She doesn't paint under her real name.'

Robin had never spoken to her about his wife's talent, but Georgiana showed no jealousy. Indeed she eulogized over the quality of the work, almost basking in the reflection of such a gifted person.

They were soon at his Rooms.

'You've got a new car!' she exclaimed, as he opened its door for her. It was a Toyota Supra Turbo 2+2 in dark blue. They sank into the comfortable bucket seats in charcoal grey leather.

'I got fed up with the little things that kept going wrong with the Rolls' he said. 'And the servicing takes so long. Ten years from now we'll probably have no car industry of our own. We can't blame the Trade Unions any longer. There must be something wrong with management.' His voice betrayed the sense of sadness he felt that the British car industry could no longer compete with those of other nations.

'I do like the smell of new leather' she said. He showed her how to alter the curvature of the back of the seat and the tilt, and she settled down in blissful comfort.

The car purred its way out of its parking space in the secure courtyard at the back of his rooms. They turned into Marylebone Road and up into Westway.

Georgiana commented on how smooth the car's suspension felt, and was very impressed by the sudden lunge of power whenever the turbo took over on accelerating. They were quickly out of the London traffic on to the A40 and then the M40. From there they headed through Marlow to Henley.

During the journey in the encapsulated confines of the car, his senses having overcome the smell of the new leather, the balmy fragrance of her Chanel perfume revived the intense desire he had felt in Helsinki.

'I cannot help being in love with you' he said. 'I don't know why.'

'I love you too. Let's just build on it without upsetting anyone.' She meant it.

They had both received invitations from Didier to his Journées in Paris. Being still in Leeds, he had placed it all in the hands of a conference agency, which had booked all facilities and accommodation at the Concorde-Lafayette. Their fares would be taken care of. Registration would be open from five o'clock on the Tuesday, 20th November, with a buffet supper that evening.

'I'm planning to take the week off as part of my annual leave and get to Paris on the Monday' said Robin. 'What are your plans?'

'I haven't discussed it with Ken yet. I don't know if he's going.'

'Well if you can go, how would you feel about being my guest on the Monday? After today, I feel like visiting the Orangerie again and seeing the Nymphéas once more. It would be nice to go to Giverny after the meeting, if there's enough time. I also want to visit a special museum in Paris.'

Georgiana had not been to the Orangerie, nor to Giverny. She like the idea of both, after having tasted Monet at the RA. She had contacts in Paris and could give them as an excuse to go early.

'I'll organise a hotel for that night and we would move the next day to Concorde. Do I book a separate room for you?'

'What for?' she replied, sounding rather dismayed. 'If I join you I want to be with you all the time!'

'Good answer! Why don't I make a provisional booking until you've discussed it with Ken?'

'OK.'

When they reached Henley, Georgiana guided him through the

urban roads to her parents' home. As they turned into the drive the well-kept garden still displayed the late blooms of a mild October.

She took him into their sitting room. On a sofa table stood a photograph of her wedding. He looked at it studiously.

'He's an attractive man, your husband' he said.

'Yes.' She was not looking at the photo. 'Shall we go upstairs?'

'Is that sensible? Your parents might not think much of it.'

He wasn't sure why he had said this. It certainly wasn't that he didn't want to go to bed with her, and they had agreed that this was not a conventional relationship. Perhaps subconsciously he was putting her own morality to the test, making sure she had overcome any guilt feelings she might have.

'Don't be silly!' she retorted. 'It's none of their business. What they don't know about they won't worry about. Anyway, it is still my room. I want you to see it. Please, let's go upstairs.'

She took him by the hand and led him towards the stairs. She sneezed twice. He knew what that meant now.

Her room was just as he had expected - elegant, feminine, tidy. The curtains and the bedspread matched the fabric of the kidney-shaped dressing table. On it, a carriage clock was ticking quietly. She had wound it on arriving that morning.

The room was an en suite with a wide shower cubicle. She had already unpacked her beauty case. A large window overlooked a neat back garden. Robin warmed to their sudden isolation from the world.

They fell into an ardent and arousing embrace, made the more hungry by the passage of time since the last. As they moved apart, her bright eyes sparkled with yearning. She reached for his tie to undo it.

'It's my turn to undress you' she said, with a happy smile of revenge.

He had less clothing on than she did and was soon naked. He turned her round to undo her balconette bra with its half cups. He dropped it off her shoulders, then slipped his fingers inside her silk French panties and drew them down to her ankles so that she could step out of them. Still standing behind her, he held her close to him, both hands round her front, clasping her breasts. She pressed her buttocks into him and felt how ready he was for her. She gave a sweet groan of acknowledgement.

He penguin-walked her to the side of the bed and she leaned over it, supported by her arms and bending fully to present herself to him. Gently he became one with her.

'Oh yes' she said. 'This is nice. Stay there.'

He felt her tighten her muscles to keep him inside her and harden him still more. Then, after a while, she relaxed to let him move forwards and backwards, doing the same with her whole body to complement his movements.

They pleasured each other in this position for over ten minutes. Finally they moved on to the bed, face to face, engaging their mouths. It was well over a quarter of an hour before they reached their climaxes, seconds apart. They rested, linked in gratification. In the silence of the room, there was only their rapid breathing and the tick-tock of the clock.

They sank together into slumber, oblivious of time. When they surfaced from the lethargy of their contentment, the waning light of early dusk had enveloped the room.

'Thank you for coming to my room' she said. 'I would have been so disappointed if you hadn't. Deprived.'

'I would not have missed it' he replied. Then he turned across her, rewarding her with a passionate and erotic kiss. It began another long love session, as fulfilling as the first.

Soon darkness had fallen and it was time to part.

'I wish you could stay all night' she said.

'It's a nice thought, but it's not possible.'

'I know. Never mind, I'll run the shower.' She got reluctantly out of bed and they showered together, soaping each other with affection and eroticism and coming close to making love all over again under the drizzle of warm water. Then it was time to get dressed and say goodbye, until Paris. As Robin passed the telephone in the hall, he noted the number.

He reached home before Louise, to find Cio-Cio on the porch waiting for someone to give her supper. He smiled at the thought that eating was the driving force of this little creature's life. He certainly would not like to change places with a neutered cat.

Cio-Cio joined him after her supper on his desk in his study. She always expressed her thanks at being fed by bringing her rag doll as a temporary present. She put it down on the very spot where he was writing down the telephone number he had memorised. He then picked up the phone and dialled it. She was surprised but overjoyed at hearing his voice again.

'How did you know the number?'

'I saw it on your phone, of course.'

'You don't miss a trick!'

'I'm glad I didn't miss you.'

'Me too.'

Cio-Cio of course assumed her master was talking to her, and acknowledged this by closing and opening her eyelids slowly and voluntarily, almost smiling. The moment he was off the phone she jumped down from his desk and went back to her basket.

The next day Georgiana got up before dawn to collect Philip. She drove straight back to Bath to be in her office by nine. She was not tired. Her mind kept going back to the previous afternoon, though it did not hinder her work. She longed for their next meeting. She would have to remember to see Ken about Paris.

CHAPTER FOURTEEN

Autumn was at its full mellowness. The mist over Regent's Park, in the early morning as Robin left for work, was always a moment of joy for him. The heavy winds had not yet visited that part of London and the trees were still hanging on to their leaves. All shades of yellow and brown dappled the landscape. Every now and then the reds splashed themselves into the midst of a changing spectrum heralding the coming desolation of winter.

In Robin's front garden, only the eucalyptus remained draped in its summer apparel of dark green leaves, with the younger, lighter ones speckling the outer garb of the tree. Here and there, a dying vermilion leaf would add its own fleck of cinnabar to that darker background, to remain on the tree throughout most of the winter.

Robin's thoughts went back to that morning at the Sibelius Monument; so different, so peaceful, so unhurried, without the bustle of his working morning. For a moment an intense wish to be there again overcame him. Once more he was puzzled by the source of such emotions. Then the previous Wednesday at Henley flashed across his mind. He saw fleetingly, in his inner eye, Georgiana's face, as bubbly as champagne. Where had he experienced that effervescence before?

The latest news was the bombshell resignation of Geoffrey Howe and the possible resulting changes in the Cabinet. Robin's pre-occupation was, however, still with the many upsetting changes at the General.

The day before, his secretary Margaret had told him about a

phone call she had received from his secretary at the hospital. It seemed that one of the other secretaries, who was suffering from gallstones, could not be referred to him because her GP had no contract with the General. She had to go elsewhere. The new internal market had destroyed past bonds between staff and employing hospitals, everywhere. Cosmetic politics had brought this about. The secretary had tried to plead her cause with the Appointments Officer, without success. He was annoyed about this and it still bugged him when he called Georgiana after his private session was over and Margaret had gone.

'We've had the same problem here since we became a Trust' she said. 'Ken's secretary lives in Keynsham and needed to be referred for a second opinion. She couldn't be seen here because her practitioner has his contract with the Infirmary in Bristol.'

'So she has to take a day off work instead of being seen at her own hospital.'

'That's right. She had to lose a further day to have some X-rays, and then another day for a follow-up appointment. It is all so stupid.'

'What does Ken feel about this?'

'He's incensed. It has meant him going without secretarial help, to the detriment of the hospital and the patients.'

'That's ridiculous.'

'I know. But there is some good news. Ken wants me to attend the whole of the Journées as he can be there for only one day.'

'Fabulous! I've already made my plans.'

'Are you going to tell me what will these plans be?'

'No. I want them to be a surprise.'

'Then I'll have to surprise you in return.' The tone of her voice was suggesting something naughty. He laughed. He was game.

* * * * * * * *

Geoffrey Dalton was away that week, so Robin had offered to see Rachel Cope and deal with her personally. On the Thursday morning she was admitted to his ward for the day. Under local anaesthesia a long arterial delivery line was inserted in her right upper chest area for her to receive her chemotherapy, twenty-four hours a day for several months, through the pump system. She was also started on a special drug to stop any clotting problems that could be induced by the line. The next day she would be started on her chemotherapy. Geoffrey or Robin would be seeing her regularly thereafter. She was certain that it would be successful, expressing full confidence in her specialists and grateful for their personal approach to her problem.

* * * * * * * * *

That next morning, the consultant staff attended a meeting convened to discuss the CE's proposal for a reduction in junior staffing, supposedly to save on manning expenditure. It was a senseless cost-cutting exercise. Robin was at his most vocal.

'Geoffrey Dalton has asked me to apologise for his absence. He's attending a breast conference, for the benefit of his patients' Robin said pointedly. 'I shall be voicing his feelings as well as mine. We both oppose reducing our complement of house officers.'

'On what grounds?' The CE was not amused.

'Grounds that may not be clear to you' was Robin's vexed reply. 'We have two officers each. Both are needed on our busy emergency days. We share a fifth who covers the unit after normal working hours on non-emergency days. Without this there would be no cover for the Unit.'

'I am not aware of this fifth requirement. Is that the case, Mr Cook?'

'I believe so' replied Ian Cook.

This vagueness annoyed Robin.

'Shouldn't you have ascertained all the facts before this meeting?'

The CE was silent.

'Well' continued Robin acidly, 'for your information, our Unit is a regional one dealing with tertiary referrals of problems from other hospitals and trusts. Not only will the new system be an added administrative burden, but these referred cases are complex, so a reduction of staffing would mean lowering the standard of care. So charging for an inferior product - since you are turning medicine into a trade - without being honest about it, amounts to fraud. Geoffrey and I are not prepared to be fraudsters.'

'You're being emotive.'

'No sir! I am interested in my patients. I am also interested in the training of my juniors. Perhaps neither interest you. You may find it more interesting to earn a bonus by cutting down patient care and stabbing the juniors. At this rate, in ten years' time, there will be a poorer NHS and little training for our juniors. That is not being emotive. That is facing hard facts.'

'Training is not my concern, it is for the colleges and the universities.'

'You're wrong' retorted Robin. 'The programmes are set by the colleges and universities, but hospitals must provide the clinical facilities for implementing them. You and your political masters are bent on denying the juniors their rightful training. It is sheer administrative arrogance. You're tilting at windmills. What the Health Service needs is good, well-informed financial managers.'

This was brutish talk. There was silence all round. No one was prepared to stand up and be counted - a common attitude in hospital seniors, most of whom are gutless. The CE had not expected this and had no answer for it. He tried to disagree, but when Robin suggested that the matter be made public, he back-pedalled.

Ian Cook kept quiet. He must have been aware of the possibility of a conflict of interest in his role as Medical Director, siding with the administration for his own reasons.

The new reforms were buying the fealty of chief executives with bonuses linked to how much they could reduce budgets. This meant curtailing clinical output and lowering standards. It would work in the short term, but eventually hospitals would be showing deficits which the taxpayer would have to meet. All the tricks in the book were being used. The Appointments Officer had been told to obtain from patients their holiday dates, ostensibly in their own interests. In fact it was to give them appointments or admission dates at times when they would not be able to take them. They would then be moved on to a fresh list. It was obscene manipulation.

After that meeting, on his way to lunch, Robin went to the gentlemen's cloakroom to use the closet. While he was there, Ian Cook and the CE came in to avail themselves of the urinals.

'I can't make an exception for Chesham' said the CE.

'Robin is a maverick' said Cook. 'He is right in saying that he attracts difficult problems which will bring in a substantial revenue. If he turns down these referrals, everybody will know and the hospital will lose money. It's more than likely that this will be leaked to the media. He's too popular with the medical and nursing staffs for this not to spread via the bush telegraph as well.'

'I'm in a cleft stick then.'

'Well, yes. You'll have a battle on your hands. I'm not sure you will win it. I am not in a position to interfere here.'

The CE did not take that up.

'I was hoping Geoffrey Dalton would have been there this morning. I was going to ask a favour of him. After the tirade from Chesham I could talk to him instead. Perhaps I could ring you at home tonight, if you don't mind?'

'Please do.'

Robin heard the pair wash their hands and leave. He chuckled, wondering what the favour was about.

When he told the story to Louise that evening, she laughed her head off. It was loo talk rather than pillow talk, she commented. Robin remarked how someone who had sold bricks and concrete products must clearly be a hard-hearted person who failed to understand the problems involved in dealing with clinical situations. How could such a money-minded person, with little therapeutic insight, possibly grasp the needs of an ill person or comprehend the intricacies and complexities of solving difficult surgical problems? Yet these were the very people entrusted with the running of a hospital to meet an ill-conceived and untested political doctrine.

The next morning, Saturday, Ian Cook was on the phone to Robin.

'The CE is seeking a favour from Geoff' he said. 'As he is away, I am being asked to seek it from you.'

'Oh yes? What is it?'

'It's his wife's sister. She's found a hard lump in her breast. She's 59. Could she be seen urgently in the breast clinic?'

'Is she local?'

'No, that's the problem. She lives in East Acton and they've referred her to the Hammersmith. Apparently they can't see her for at least three weeks.'

'Well, well, look who's talking. Why doesn't he just ring Number Ten and ask for an exception?'

'I thought you would say that. I take it you're not prepared to help?'

'I didn't make the rules. I'm told that one of our medical secretaries was refused a similar favour a few days back. What's sauce for the goose, and all that.'

'What about seeing her privately then?'

'I can't see that working either. If she needs surgery and perhaps radiotherapy, she will still have to go to the Hammersmith as per the internal market, unless all her care is done privately. I'm not one to play this sort of game just for the money.'

'I see. This is making it awkward for me. It won't help being difficult.'

'It is not a question of being difficult. If we hadn't been pushed into these stupid reforms it would have been different. Under the old system I would have bent backwards to help any member of staff or their family. Now it's merchandising. This is not my choice. The CE is prepared to be bought - I am not.'

Ian Cook had little else to say. He knew he could not budge Robin. He would have much to explain to his new boss. He had made his bed, and now he had to lie in it.

CHAPTER FIFTEEN

Robin had left it as a surprise where they would stay the first night in Paris before joining Didier at Concorde-Lafayette. Georgiana, always dominated by the fear of missing planes, had prevailed upon him to arrive early at Heathrow, so they had a good hour to while away before their flight was called. She had plans for the time.

'Will you be my guest for a special treat?' she asked.

'That sounds good. But you're meant to be my guest.'

'Not until we get to France.'

She walked him past the arcades of duty-free shops to the circular counter of the champagne seafood bar.

'This is where I want to spoil you' she said.

'We can now both overindulge. It's starters for the day.' The eyes he was coming to like more and more shone with added brilliance. She was looking forward to the rest of the day.

She told him Ken was planning a symposium in Bath and thought that he and Didier would be useful speakers. Ken had given her the task of setting it up on a suitable date early the coming year and choosing appropriate subjects. She felt proud to be allocated this assignment, but thought it wise to await the success of the Journées before getting to work. Ken was flying to Paris the next day and could only attend one day of the current meeting, but he wanted Georgiana to stay for the full programme and report back to him. It gave her carte blanche to be with Robin.

Robin suggested on the plane that they took the Air France coach to the terminal, which was in the same block as the hotel.

'I'd like to call in to see if they could book adjoining rooms for the next night' he told her.

'I'll go along with that, but the rooms must already have been block booked.'

'Probably, but the French understand charm' was his smiling reply.

Reception confirmed their bookings of the next day and Robin chatted up the receptionist in French and persuaded her to organise inter-connecting rooms.

'You're a philanderer!' Georgiana teased him.

'Philandering as an overt means to an end is the most useful inter-gender social lubricant there is.'

'As long as that's all it is, I'll go along with it.'

'Jealousy will get you nowhere' Robin mused with a twinkle in his eyes.

The concierge hailed a taxi and Robin instructed the driver so that Georgiana couldn't hear. It was a short ride down the Avenue de la Grande Armée and on to the top of the Champs Elysées. She remained curious about where he was taking her, and he played on her curiosity. After three hours together she was none the wiser.

When the taxi stopped outside the George V, the glint in her eyes revealed her elation. The doorkeeper recognised Robin. It was one of his favourite hotels. 'Soyez le bienvenu, Monsieur Chesham' he said. Robin shook hands with him. He had not seen Robin with anyone else at the hotel before, but he kept his own counsel.

'You're pampering me' Georgiana said softly.

'I'm spoiling myself by having company here for the first time.' This was true.

A concierge - one of the 'Clefs D'Or' - courteously invited G to sit down while Robin was booking in. Her eyes took in the full elegance of the foyer with its attractive marble floor and discreetly-placed small silk carpets. Behind the reception desk, a superb tapestry hung the full width of the wall. Opulence and luxury oozed from every corner.

After signing in, Robin went over to the head concierge and collected something from him. A call boy stood nearby waiting to take their luggage and see them to their room. He was impeccably dressed in a dark uniform with shining brass buttons down the front and a well-laundered collar matching his cylindrical hat carrying the hotel name across it. On the left breast of his jacket was embroidered the hotel logo: two intertwined mirrored Gs, linked by a Roman five and surmounted by a royal crown.

'As you can see, I made certain that everyone carried your initials on their uniform' he said teasingly.

Georgina had not noticed this, but she rose to the occasion. 'I would have expected nothing less' she smiled.

'I'll take you to see some of the salons while the boy deals with our luggage' said Robin. They walked down a short corridor. The Salon Régence, of a partially octagonal shape, was austere with its panelling and matching wooden mantelpiece, but it nonetheless had a cosy atmosphere. It could take a large round table for less formal meetings or intimate dining occasions. In the next room, the Louis XIII Suite, a velvety, colourful Aubusson tapestry hung above a late Renaissance-style mantelpiece and the Louis fauteuils. Robin took her to the other side to show her the bar where a harpist would frequently play and where the burgundy upholstery contrasted with a light gold and pale green carpet.

It was gone five o'clock when they got to their suite on the first floor. The furniture and general style was an exquisite mixture of antique and modern. The walls, in pale lemon, with juxtaposed papered panels matching the upholstery, gave the room an impression of space and lightness. This was further enhanced by wide double mirrors as doors to a large wardrobe. Alongside the whole width of the queen-size bed, a long, six-legged upholstered stool, the height of the bed, carried two end cushions. It almost gave the impression of an unboxed ottoman. The room opened into a green bathroom with a painted scenery above the bath, reflecting itself in a large mirror over the hand basin.

Near the French window, on a low table between two armchairs, were red roses in a vase with a card carrying just the words: 'with love'. There was champagne on ice and two flutes waiting for them. Everything had been thought of to pamper Robin's guest and turn a short leisure break into something much more memorable.

She placed her arms around his neck and covered him in kisses, finishing on his mouth. 'You spoil me too much' she said. 'I have no means of returning so much affection and thought.'

'You more than reward me with your love. You throw the whole of yourself into it - in all possible ways.'

'You make me want you all the time' she replied. 'I long for you to possess me.'

'Let's drink to that.' He uncorked the bottle and poured the champagne. They clinked their glasses and he dropped a tender kiss on her lips as they drank to each other.

'What are your plans now?' she enquired, and sneezed.

He laughed.

'The sneeze could be a clue!'

'You may get a surprise' she rebutted him with an enigmatic smile. 'Maybe we should have a nice soak. The journey has made me feel sticky.'

'I'll join you then, if that's what you want.'

'What do you think?' she enquired, with a mischievous raising of her right eyebrow.

The whirlpool bath was wider and longer than most. They sat facing each other, his outstretched legs on either side of her body with her open thighs across his. Her nakedness had aroused an obvious reaction in him. As he unwrapped the rose-scented soap, she reached her right hand across to him.

'I'll have that' she said. She did not lean forward to wash it, but to stroke it expertly. And then, that task completed, she bent down towards him and applied her full mouth to stimulate him. He writhed with pleasure.

After some five or six minutes he said: 'I think he is feeling hungry. Let's get out of the bath.'

They dried each other and moved back to the bedroom. Robin pulled the long stool away from the foot of the bed, discarded one cushion and laid her on it with her legs dangling down on either side of the ottoman. He stood across her and bent down, kissing her on her mouth. Then he moved his kisses down her body until he reached her spread-out, drawn-up thighs. She found his tongue exciting, arousing and disturbingly erotic, the more so because she could follow every movement of his in the double mirrors.

'That's nice. That's so nice!' she said, luxuriating in every touch.

It is a common belief that lovemaking is instinctive. Yet while the urge is undoubtedly instinctive, the execution is not. Sexuality is an appetite determined by an inner chemistry leading one person to be physically driven to another, regardless of gender, and culminating in covalence. Perhaps our genes determine that behaviour and promote the attachment. For that bond to sustain a coupling permanency, it must constantly be enriched, but above all its harmony must be appreciated. The urge may lead to the trial run, but that simply bears the imprint of the novice. It is, on such occasion, a biological exercise devoid of the finesse of pre-knowledge. The self-analytical performer can learn by trial and error and excel eventually. However, it demands time. In the uninitiated, it carries the damage of inexperience, and the recreation may become monotonous, unchanging and unfulfilling. For the studious, all forms of art are better taught and refined by tutored execution.

None of this is instinctive. Good lovemaking is a self-recreational art that requires the cognate to exalt it. If not taught it simply withers through dull repetition. Georgiana's analytical intelligence on this occasion communicated to her a new pleasure that she would commit to her recollection of the act and seek to develop whenever possible. It was not sexual instinct but sexual erudition. She enjoyed both the teacher and the lesson. Nor was it just physical gratification. She needed to express her love in a manner that was private and personal, and in return was rewarded by a cultured response.

He met her craving to be invaded. She moved her body from side to side to savour every second of this new experience. Suddenly she yelled out: 'Darling, darling, quick, quick!' He burst profusely inside her as she shrieked with more delight, her body finally relaxing completely and stilling itself in full sycophancy with his.

Having brought each other to culmination, they returned to their glasses and enjoyed fondling each other in their uncovered state, sipping their champagne.

'You haven't told me where we're going tonight' she said.

'You'll find out in good time' he replied, teasing her to despair.

'I've got to know what to wear.'

'Let's say semi-formal.'

She knew he was driving her to provocation only to enjoy her the more later, and he watched her put on her rousing lingerie, knowing he would revel in it again when they came back.

They walked towards the Champs Elysées, crossed on to the other side and within a few metres turned into an open wide lobby. It was the entrance to the Lido. It was the reservation to this that Robin had been collecting when Georgiana had watched him talking to the Head Clef d'Or. She had never been to such a place, and it would be yet another experience for her. He warned her that the meal would not be a gourmet one and that the champagne was not the best, but the show would be exciting. And it was. It ended with a mini helicopter flying right across the audience on to the stage.

Between courses they went down to the stage to dance. Robin spoke to the band leader and they were soon dancing to Lara's Theme, harnessed tenderly to each other and lost in memories. Later, they took to the floor to Latin American tunes which they both enjoyed. If the rumba puts into rhythm the language of love, the tango does the same for the promise of seduction and the expression of forbidden love - and both promise and expression were there when they got back to the George V, to be once more lost to the world and to belong only to each other.

CHAPTER SIXTEEN

The next morning they had no need to rush out of bed, so they spent a couple of hours enjoying each other's company before getting up to enjoy breakfast on room service and then to soak in an enjoyable bath.

They left their suitcases with the Head Concierge to collect them later that afternoon on their way to Concorde-Lafayette, and then made once more for the Champs Elysées.

'Are you happy to walk a kilometre?' Robin asked.

She was game. She liked walking, and there was so much to explore on foot in that part of Paris.

They crossed to the other side of the Avenue, made for Rue de Berri, which took them at its far end to the Boulevard Haussmann, named after Napoleon III's greatest préfet and one of the world's finest town planners. Few who visit Paris are aware that without his genius they would not have had the Bois de Boulogne, or the Opera House, or the 'grands boulevards' under which he ran tunnels to provide the city with its water supply, its drainage system and now its many essential utility services. The streets of Paris do not get dug up as frequently as our London ones, thanks to these égouts.

They crossed the boulevard to its northern side, where Robin was planning to take his willing guest - a house not dissimilar in its concept to the Wallace Collection, but far more luxurious, unclustered and sumptuously French. It was not freely open to the public at that time, but organised as he always was, Robin had written to the administrateur to be allowed to visit it that morning.

Before leaving London he had kept Georgiana guessing about his three surprises. His second was now the Musée Jacquemart-André. There was a third one yet to come.

To the collector of art and the lover of elegant surroundings, there are few places as prestigious as this house-cum-museum. To appreciate its neo-classical architecture and façade, one needs to cast one's imagination to the Paris of the 1850s when the site was the Plaine Monceau laid out to Napoleon III's specifications to become the most opulent and privileged quarter of Paris. To Edouard André and his wife Nélie Jacquemart, there could not have been a better site for their grand residence. It was a small palace of exquisite design like those found in Kensington Palace Gardens, which they left, at their deaths, to the Institut de France.

A delightful statuette by Jean Baptiste Pigalle in the entrance lobby welcomes the visitor and leads him to a marble hall with a geometrical tiling of Greek crosses in reverse swastikas. A breathtaking double 'escalier d'honneur' takes one to a balcony suspended by columns with Corinthian chapters. Busts, statues, carpets, pristine pieces of furniture and resplendent chandeliers fill the eyes. On the magnificently panelled walls, tapestries from Gobelins hold one's attention, while cloisonné incense burners and Chinese vases in splendid blues or greens catch the breath with their delicate floral decorations.

Georgiana was all eyes. Above all, the spacious rooms and the tasteful display of furniture and of well-proportioned outstanding paintings made it more of a house than a museum. They stayed there for all of two hours and could have stayed all day, but it was half past one and Robin's third surprise was now waiting for her.

He hailed a taxi, destination 15 Quai de Tournelle. The address meant nothing to Georgiana, who smiled back questioningly. It drove past Notre Dame and turned behind it over the bridge across

Ile St Louis on to the Rive Gauche, where it stopped outside an unremarkable building which hardly betrayed the fact that it housed one of the most famous restaurants in Paris. Perhaps the Café Anglais was no longer the finest gourmet place of the Cité, but it was pregnant with history, having had its heyday during the Second Empire when it still bore the name of Café Anglais. There Dumas had set the scene for one of his novels, while almost a century previously, Madame de Sévigné, in her indomitable study of the French fashionable society of the 17th century, had made the place famous. There too, the fork had been used for the first time as a new culinary instrument.

The entrance at the corner of the building led them to a unique piece of history on the ground floor: a table with its original setting of silver cutlery, crystal glasses and Limoges blue and white china. There on the 7th June 1867, at that dinner table, had sat Bismarck, the Junker prime minister, in company with his Prussian King, Wilhelm I, Emperor of Germany. The year before, he had excluded Austria from German affairs, effectively destroying the Hapsburg dynasty. Bismarck's career had previously taken him to St Petersburg as Ambassador, where he had gained the friendship and confidence of Czar Alexander II. It was thus no coincidence that the latter was also at the table with his Czarevitch. Bismarck was quietly plotting to isolate Napoleon III and, having unified the North German States, he was now seeking to bring into that confederation the Southern German states by frightening them with the fears of invasion by France. This was a shrewd move, as France had no allies at the time and its artillery was hopelessly out of date. French cannons were still made of brass, while the Germans had modern steel ones. Four years later, there resulted a very short Franco-German war in which France lost Alsace-Lorraine and Germany became unified, the treaty of unification being signed in Versailles. France had learned the lesson of being isolated and quickly moved in the direction of an Entente Cordiale with England. The Prince of Wales, later Edward VII, was to visit Paris frequently to cement the Entente, aside from certain more colourful interests. Naturally he found his way to the Café Anglais.

They took the lift to the top floor. An old fashioned 'ascenseur', bearing all the architectural features of the Grand Siècle, delivered them slowly to the penthouse restaurant with its panelled walls: the Tour D'Argent.

Robin had carefully reserved, well in advance, a window table beautifully laid out with Limoges china and crystal glasses. From there, the view over Paris, north of the Seine, is spectacular. There can be no better view of the Gothic architecture of Nôtre Dame and its massive buttresses. The whole grandeur of the French capital offers itself to one's eyes, not just Nôtre Dame but beyond it to the Palais de Justice and further afield the Louvre and the Tuileries. It was a cloudless day and the soft autumn sun in a pale blue sky cast its gentle warmth on them without being blinding. They felt extremely happy. Their intimacy was away from the eyes of the world. She remembered the restaurant in Helsinki, placed her left hand, palm up, across the table to call for his right hand and said lovingly: 'Thank you.'

'What about a Kir Royal?' he suggested.

'Volontiers.'

Robin pointed out to her the restaurant owner. He was immaculately dressed, dandy fashion, carrying his traditional cornflower on his left lapel.

The menu arrived. The sommelier brought the Kir Royal and the wine list. It was not an extensive menu, but everything on it carried the stamp of quality.

'What do you suggest?' she asked unpretentiously.

'Well, fish is excellent. Either the sea bream or the pike. Their quenelles de brochet is their specialty. You should try it.'

'And what are you going to have?'

'I've had their quenelles before. I think I shall try their Crabe Lagardère.'

'What next?'

'I have brought you here specially to taste what they are famous for, their pressed canard flambé.'

He explained to her how in 1890 the restaurant's distinguished chef had produced this flambé duck dish to be first served to the Prince of Wales. From then on it was the talk of the town. That ritual has remained ever since and she would see it re-enacted by their table. She thought it exciting and accepted the invitation.

He scanned the wine list, which was exhaustive. The restaurant was reputed for its wines and was believed to have a stock of some quarter of a million bottles, many over a century old. He showed her the list. 1985 had produced some powerful white burgundies and maconnais, and he looked at a Montagny 1er cru and a St Véran. A Côte de Beaune 1982 would be soft and non-tannic and would accompany the duck well. Without affectation, he sought the sommelier's advice. He proposed a good 1985 Puligny-Montrachet and a gentle and sweet flavoured 1982 Nuits St Georges. They both agreed on these.

After the first course, they watched the duck being prepared. A card carrying the number of the duck was placed in front of them while it was being carved. Carcass and legs went into the press, to be crushed after red wine had been poured on it. A rich sauce trickled out of the press to anoint the breasts of duck after their endowment with brandy ready for the flambé ritual - searing at its most elegant.

The meal was so enjoyable that they were surprised to find that it was nearly four o'clock when they left the table. It was time to think of the conference. Even so, on their way out, they visited the cellars with their vast array of wines and its museum of the history of wine. It reminded Georgiana of Harveys' museum in Bristol, but it was more comprehensive and more international in its range of items.

They stopped at the George V and were shortly afterwards registering with the conference and settling down in their interlinked rooms, where they reminisced about their pleasurable day while sorting out their slides in preparation for their lectures over the next two days.

Their holiday interlude was now over. Their quality time together would be limited, that 20th day of November having passed too quickly for them.

CHAPTER SEVENTEEN

Bob Hirst arrived just in time for the welcome dinner of the speakers, scheduled for eight o'clock that Tuesday. He had driven from Leeds to Birmingham and flown from there to Paris, where Didier had arranged for him to be met at Charles de Gaulle. It was the least he could have done for his closest colleague and friend. With his impeccable French politeness, he had not wanted to start the dinner before all his guests had arrived.

There had been pre-dinner drinks while they were waiting for Bob. Georgiana and Robin were in fact the last ones to arrive before him. There was a good reason for this. They had been scanning the TV channels; Georgiana, whose parents supported Michael Heseltine, wanted to find out what had happened earlier that day in the House of Commons with the ballot for the leadership contest of the Conservative Party. She had not been able to satisfy her curiosity until a newsflash showed Mrs Thatcher coming out to speak to the Press after the European meeting at Versailles. The results were a bombshell.

It had all started three weeks before, on 1st November, when Geoffrey Howe resigned as Leader of the House and Deputy Prime Minister and then in his resignation speech a week later had savaged his Prime Minister on her attitude to Europe and the Free Market. He had repeatedly been belittled by her and had put up with her barbs time and again, as well as her acrobatics over European Union. Her xenophobia had been sickening. For public consumption she would constantly protest about every aspect of the European Act, but when the moment of endorsement came she dutifully signed everything placed in front of her. She had, after all, signed the single European Act. Howe's resignation had been the signal for a contest for the leadership of the party.

The dinner - almost a banquet - was a convivial occasion with much jollity. Didier, at his table of eight, had assembled his English speakers and many from the group in Helsinki, including Lars Nordin and Carl Rieger. Though Ken Taylor was not a speaker, Didier out of courtesy had invited him. He was going back to Bath the next day once the afternoon session was over. As an affable gesture for Didier's cross-channel friends, there was port on the table.

As the decanter was being passed round in the conventional direction, Bob Hirst asked if anyone had heard the result of the Tory ballot.

'Yes' Georgiana leapt in with the news. 'Thatcher defeated Heseltine, but with not enough votes for an outright victory. So there will be a second ballot.'

'Unless she resigns' interrupted Robin.

Bob and Ken were inveterate Thatcherites, feeling they understood what she stood for. 'There will be pressure on Heseltine to stand down' said Bob hopefully.

'I'm not so sure' said Georgiana. 'He has a very strong following in Henley. My parents live there and they think very highly of him. Their feeling is that the Conservative Party needs a new leader. The voting seems to have suggested this.'

'Well, I think differently' Bob replied. 'It may well be that a third person will need to be pushed forward.'

'That would be a mistake' said Robin. 'Who is there left? She has Dyno-Rodded every sensible person there was in the Government. Douglas Hurd appears old-fashioned and too much a product of an ankylosed establishment to have the necessary support. John Major lacks vision. He is politically manipulative enough to get a degree of support and keep himself in power. With the new ideas that are now required he won't last long. One thing is certain: if Thatcher stays, the Tories will lose the next election. As a party which is so interested in itself and the advantages of money, it will not keep a leader who's likely to sink it. They have never done so in the past.'

'But why would they want to get rid of her?' Didier enquired.

'She has crucified the middle classes with her lack of reality and her obsession with free marketing' Robin continued. 'By 1982 a quarter of the manufacturing industry in the UK had been destroyed, and it will probably never recover. Interest rates and inflation are running high and have eroded the incomes of the middle classes. Young people are finding it difficult to afford a decent house. The Poll Tax is the most stupid idea that was ever thought of.'

'Come come' said Ken. 'The trade unions were destroying the country, public expenditure was increasing and the previous government could no longer cope.'

'I don't deny that' Robin replied. 'But whichever party had come to power in 1979 would have had to do something about the way the unions had been taken over by the militants. The government of the day had too small a majority to take them on. The huge majority won by the Tories was what made this possible, not necessarily the Prime Minister. By then the Labour Party had become unelectable, and Michael Foot simply made them more so.'

'I go along with this' said Bob. 'But who else other than Thatcher would have dared take on the unions?'

The main worry of those present was the way the police or 'Maggie's boot boys' had been used in a quasi-military way to crush the strike against the Murdoch empire during the Wapping dispute with the 'refuseniks'. Furthermore, the Murdoch press had supported the Tories during the 1979 election. It had probably increased the grip of a powerful press baron on a weak body politic, while making the public see the police as enemies rather than friends. Rioting, like the urban violence at Toxteth in 1981, would increase. Power, like poverty, breeds criminals. What was being used as a dubious political solution could well, in time, bring about a major social problem. Democracy suffers from being militarised.

The discussion went on for a while, Lars Nordin and Carl Rieger describing the views held in their respective countries. Didier seemed very quiet.

"You like her, don't you Didier?" said Robin. "Your countrymen have a high opinion of La dame de fer.'

'No no!' Didier vehemently replied. 'Only the right-wing papers take this attitude. France is a centrist nation. The thinking professionals tend to be left of centre. The tradesmen are those that are vocal on the right of centre, but they are not a majority. France has a socialist president for that reason.'

He was getting very excited about the non-thinking tradesmen of France and had no great love for the Conservative Party.

'C'est une petite bourgeoise qui sent encore de l'épice' he concluded.

Ken goaded him in a friendly manner. If she no longer had a Praetorian Guard to keep her in power, someone else would have to take her place.

'Who would you like as a new leader then?' asked Ken.

'There may be other postulants, such as your neo-communist Basque minister' Didier suggested.

'We don't have communist Basque ministers!' Ken replied, affronted.

'Oh yes. I have read about him. He hides his background by being right wing and more British than the Monarchy. Now, what's his name? Oh, I remember: Portaloo.'

There were guffaws of laughter. Didier could not see what was so funny.

Robin explained. 'Portaloo is the brand name of a portable toilet system, like those you see on building sites. I think you mean Portillo."

The laughter gave some relief, but there was genuine concern that at a time of worrying international squabbles, Britain would be in the throes of reshaping the Government. There was a growing antipathy to Thatcherism, the more so that a Cabinet paying lip service to the sanctity of human rights in the world, with a finger pointing at China, Iraq, Romania or the crumbling Yugoslavia, was quite happy to forget all about it when the interests of the city financial moguls had to be safeguarded.

The port had now been round several times, and everyone was in a very sociable mood. They soon forgot their political differences. Robin, anxious to get back to Georgiana, suggested it was time to retire.

The next day the conference soon got under way and was very well attended. Didier had chosen topical subjects, as well as problems to be solved. Georgiana gave her presentation in the afternoon, and it was faultless. Ken Taylor took great pride in the reception it got and the many questions it engendered, some of which he chose to answer. Earlier on, during the lunch break, he had enlisted both Didier and Robin for his forthcoming symposium in Bath, though the exact time was still undetermined. He would leave it to Georgiana to contact them.

Robin and Georgiana had little time together during these two days. They were sensible enough not to display the closeness that united them. Evenings were sociable, but both had good reason not to be the last ones to leave.

By the time the conference was over, they had spent three nights together and their hunger for each other had not diminished in the least, nor was their corporeal tryst any less than at any time before.

They felt a sadness when they left the hotel after the conference, not quite certain when they would be with each other again. They had, however, some time together as they flew back to London. Lack of time had robbed them the chance of seeing the Orangerie or going to Giverny. It could be a pleasure postponed.

They sat together with an empty third seat in the row. Equally empty was the row in front of them, so they could chat freely about the previous days together. It was evident to them that a very strong bond united them. It was not a mere passing attraction. Robin wanted to ascertain how Georgiana still felt about it and if it was disturbing her emotionally in anyway. He said he would be frank with her and expected an equally frank response.

'No, I feel very at ease with our relationship as it is' she retorted. 'Philip and I are very much involved with each other, and I'm sure it is a companionship for life.'

Robin remained silent for a moment.

'Perhaps you want to know more' she mused. But Robin did not take the cue, so she continued. 'We are very compatible physically, though perhaps I am the more demanding and tend often to make the first move. But this suits us both and doesn't need to change.'

'I am glad to hear that' was Robin's reply, 'but I hope I am not disturbing you in any other way.'

'No, you won't break us up, it's a very stable partnership. It's just that you have enhanced my quality of life and added another dimension to it in all ways, intellectual, emotional and physical. You're a long distance runner in bed and that's totally new to me. I am used to shorter distances. I like the new experience and I would not want to be robbed of you. You are well beyond two standard deviations, I imagine.'

Robin laughed at this statistical evaluation of his style.

'I appreciate your frankness. I'm equally attached to Louise and couldn't think of life without her. I am still puzzled about what made me fall in love with you. Thinking about it took me back to the girl I first fell in love with at the beginning of my career. I had wanted her for life, but it didn't work out that way. I had to repress a powerful emotion and then find a new set of feelings for someone else when Louise came into my life. Somehow, I am now finding in you some sort of reincarnation of my very first emotion, repressed for so long. It's different to the one that attaches me to Louise. It seems so strange and takes me back so far away. Nonetheless, it has made me fall in love with you. I hope you understand. I'm not making comparisons.'

He held her hand, leaned towards her and kissed her forehead.

'Thank you. I'm glad we can talk about ourselves this way. I share your emotional intelligence.'

Georgiana wanted to know if there was anything else in their relationship that concerned him.

'I have no concerns' he answered 'except perhaps that if at any time our relationship leaked out, I wonder how we would deal with it.'

'I don't think we need to worry about that. Perhaps I could look at it in reverse. What I mean is that if I thought Philip was having a liaison of some sort, it would be silly of me to raise it. It would be counterproductive. If I forced him to admit it, I would have to live with the knowledge of its certainty. Equally so, if having brought it into the open he decided to give it up, I would still have to live with that knowledge. What advantage would this have? It seems to me sensible not to rock the boat. It's better to accept the doubt and continue to cement and enjoy an unbroken relationship, provided I have not been robbed of anything. I would rather have loyalty than fidelity. I think that if Philip had doubts about me he would act in the same way.'

'I am glad to hear this. I would do exactly what you would. I feel certain that Louise would do the same. It's a question of taking an intelligent view about it. We would not be the first ones to realise that there are such things as parallel emotions.'

He paused and smiled affectionately. 'Can we go on being in love with each other?'

'I would not wish it to be otherwise.'

They were soon at Heathrow. They felt disconsolate at parting, but they knew that happier circumstances would soon bring them together again.

'See you soon in Bath, I hope' were Georgiana's encouraging parting words.

It had been a dialogue between two perceptive beings displaying the sensibility of emotional intelligence - a rare trait even among educated professionals. It would remain the foundation of their robust bond.

CHAPTER EIGHTEEN

The next day, Monday 26th, the House of Commons was in turmoil as it awaited the news of the ballot for the election of a new Tory leader. Whoever was to become the next Prime Minister, it would not be someone elected by the nation but by the party in power, this being the constitutional right of party members.

The election was expected to be essentially a contest between John Major and Michael Heseltine, though all leaks were pointing to Major having the advantage. He had played his cards well by backing so-called Thatcherism, whether he believed in it or not.

The results gave him 185 votes, Heseltine 131 and Hurd 56 - two votes short of a winning margin. Clearly Heseltine would be unlikely to make up the difference if there were yet another ballot, so he immediately withdrew his candidature. Therefore Major was elected, though without a majority vote.

We are a country with an obsolescent political system, and our adversarial legal system is equally archaic. The result is that we do not have a constitution that clearly defines what we can expect. Neither Whitehall nor Westminster will ever change Britain's attitude to politics unless they change themselves. Their systems have no structure for a sweeping political reconstruction.

Neither of the two main parties has the guts to be radical enough to alter the electoral system to a more democratic one. If Tory policies fail, they do not change them. Instead they change their leader. Perhaps this is because ministerial jobs are filled in a haphazard way and ministers rarely have any expertise in the post they fill. They hold them for their own aggrandisement. As a result, when policies go wrong, the Cabinet's manipulative 'senators' and the external grandees pull their daggers out and stab their Caesar in the back. Margaret Thatcher had to experience this. When she came to announce her resignation in the House, the news by then being in the public domain, her party cheered her and waved their papers. But quite rightly the Opposition benches shouted 'hypocrites'. Such is the world of British politics.

On Thursday 22nd November, after the Prime Minister had announced her resignation, Georgiana, still at the conference, had rung her father from Paris and had a long discussion with him. She had reported it to Robin that afternoon.

'Dad is a member of the local Conservative Party. They all support Michael Heseltine. They agree with Geoffrey Howe that Thatcher was dividing the country and the party. The opinion polls throughout the year had given Labour around a twenty per cent lead. The Conservatives had lost Eastbourne to the Liberals with just about the same swing and had been third in the Bradford election. They're heading for defeat at the next election. Meanwhile, they are still split over Europe.'

'Have you read Heseltine's book on Europe?' asked Robin. 'It's superbly written and all embracing.'

'No, but Dad has and he counts himself a Europhile. He is in banking and finance and was not too keen on Britain joining the ERM. On the other hand, he thinks it was wrong of the PM to run down the EMU in Rome and give her own inflexible view that Britain will never join the single currency without the country having its say. Heseltine would not have behaved that way. Furthermore, it does not appear rational for her to join Lawson and Home in their support of the ERM, which is meant to harmonise European currency to bring about monetary union, and then disregard the EMU.'

'But Madam is not likely to let Heseltine have a free run now. Her viciousness will come out. The latest news is that Major and Hurd have thrown their hats in the ring.'

'That's bad news' she said. 'The Tories being so split, they will go for a weak candidate and compromise as usual. Their voting support in the country is slowly shrinking.'

On his return from Paris Robin had asked Louise about her views, both on the awkward way the Tories elect their leaders and on the electoral system.

'When he was a minister, my father always held that the Tories would never alter the first-past-the-post system for any other, whether proportional representation or an alternative vote system' she said. 'They fear that these two systems could keep them out of power for long periods. So they rarely change their innate policies. They like money. They like the power it gives.'

'You're probably right. Politics is a religion for them. They believe they have a divine right to govern. It has been ordained for them by their God of wealth.'

The election of John Major as Tory leader of course made him Prime Minister as well. He now had to deal with the situation in the Middle East as Saddam Hussein continued to defy the United Nations and hold British hostages, whom Tony Benn was trying to liberate.

A coalition of some 32 nations, including several Arab states, were building up their forces in Saudi Arabia and carefully planning their assault on Iraq. Perhaps Saddam thought all this was bluff. The coalition forces, once Christmas was over and the climate made it propitious, would be ready to strike. All efforts were being made to avert a war, but Saddam remained defiant and the world held its breath. Would all the nations involved agree how to deal with him, or would they have to appease all the others not involved once they had defeated him? The United Nations Organisation has the habit of emasculating itself.

CHAPTER NINETEEN

While her husband had been in Paris, Louise had rung her sister-in-law Linda to find out what she was doing for Christmas. In January Robin had lost his eldest brother in the same way he had lost his father. Both had been struck by an unexpected heart attack, though they had been in every other way active and well - a thunderbolt coming out of a clear blue sky.

Robin's brother, like his father, had suffered from recurrent indigestion and in both cases it was shown to be caused by a duodenal ulcer. Otherwise, he was an essentially healthy person who had never smoked and was a keen squash player, good enough to compete at county level. Robin had kept him informed of new knowledge about his ulcer problem and he had been among the first ones to receive a curative treatment in his brother's unit at the General. It had changed his life insofar as he could subsequently eat and drink as he liked, and he had felt better than ever before.

His loss before the age of sixty had been a major blow to the family. His only child - a son - had married and settled in Canada. Linda was now on her own. The months that followed her husband's death had been painful, and both Louise and Robin had visited her frequently to offer support in her grief. It was the little things that she had found painful. How to empty his wardrobe; what to do with his toolbox; which of the two cars to keep. Then there was the loneliness of a double bed. She had not been prepared for her loss. For the first time in some thirty years she would be alone for Christmas. Louise had therefore invited her to join them, and she had agreed. Robin was delighted by the news.

'When's she coming?'

'She's coming on the Monday and she'll spend Christmas Day and Boxing Day with us.'

Robin was saddened by the thought that in their guest en suite, with its wide double bed, she would feel all on her own for the first time at Christmas. He would also be missing his brother. It would, however, give her the chance of seeing their two children, Rodney and Lucille, if they were joining them.

'Have you spoken to the children?' he asked Louise.

Rodney had spoken to his mother during Robin's absence. He was working in Oxford in the Department of Astrophysics, having obtained a Mathematics Honours degree with distinction that year. Louise and Robin had visited him on his 22nd birthday and seen the little flat he had moved into on a short lease. It was a snug cosy home reflecting part of the cultural heritage of his parents, and a contrast to the spartan first home Louise and Robin had had when hospital juniors lived on a pittance. Robin, having lost his father while a teenager, had no parental help. His eaglet was now building its own eyrie, and it gave him a great sense of paternal pride.

'Rodney is coming to see us next weekend' said Louise.

'That's good. I haven't seen the boy since they came in September.'

Rodney was visiting them ostensibly to ask if he could 'borrow' the writing desk in his bedroom for his flat. Above all, he wanted to ask his parents, discreetly, if his girlfriend Zoe could join him over Christmas, as her parents would be away on a cruise to celebrate their 25th wedding anniversary. She was in her final year at Somerville College and would be on her own.

He took the matter up with his father on the Sunday morning, having realised that the guest room was already spoken for.

'Where are we going to put her up?' Robin enquired, tongue in cheek.

'She can share my room' was Rodney's meek reply.

'And your single bed?'

'She'll have to put up with it until the guest room is free' Rodney replied.

'I'll have to discuss it with your mother.'

'Dad!' Rodney retorted in an injured voice. 'We sleep together in my flat. What's the difference?'

'I don't doubt that. I am not concerned by it. It is simply that your aunt will be with us and we must not upset her.'

Robin paused for a few seconds, realising that his son looked unhappy.

'I'm not being priggish' he said. 'It would be silly for me to think that you don't sleep with your girlfriends. I did the same. Your mother and I lived together before we were married, but we didn't impose it on our parents.'

'I don't want to do that, Dad' Rodney replied with some humility. 'I realise I shouldn't have said as much to her, but I didn't know someone had bagged the guest room.'

'Don't worry about it for the moment. I'll talk to Mum and we'll see what we can do.'

Before closing their chat, Robin wanted to know more about Rodney's relationship with the girl. Was it just experimental? Was there an emotional bond, or was it just physical gratification? Did the emotions follow the act or precede it? Was he in love with her, or did he just love her? Who took responsibility for risk?

Rodney was not in the least offended by being asked such personal questions. He had many times heard his father's views on sex and had taken them on board. He had all the answers. The intimacy was still more marked at the physical level and they enjoyed it. They had not yet reached the stage when they would feel that the emotional and intellectual relationship could be lifelong. It was too early. If they realised it would not last, they would part company amicably and not stand in each other's way, so as to allow other relationships to develop.

Robin was happy with that. Father and son were on the same wavelength.

Robin conferred with Louise about it while she was getting lunch ready.

'I'm not sure it's a good idea' she said.

'We mustn't upset the boy's Christmas. It would be hard for him to be with his girlfriend on their own in Oxford during that week. It's nice that he feels this is still his home.'

'I accept that. On the other hand, we mustn't upset your sister-in-law.'

Robin agreed with this. Louise, like him, was broad-minded. They had brought up their children liberally and neither harboured prudish misgivings about their physical proclivities. Robin thought he would reinforce Louise's invitation by phoning his sister-in-law to say how delighted he was that she could join them for Christmas. He also used the call to mention that Rodney was bringing his girlfriend. Would she be offended if they shared a room?

To his great relief, he heard that they had accepted the same thing when their son had brought his girlfriend before they got engaged. She had long come to terms with such happenings. Rodney was jubilant at the news and could not wait to ring Zoe about it, though he was going to see her very soon.

When they told Lucille, their daughter, of Rodney's request, she admitted to having an intimate boyfriend. However, he was expected to join his parents for the festive season, while she wanted to be with hers and see her cat. So the whole Chesham family would be together for Christmas.

* * * * * * * *

Rachel Hudson had sent Robin a large box of chocolates, with an equally large Christmas card expressing her thanks for what he had done for her. It was a hard time for her, as she was tied to her home during her months of chemotherapy treatment. Much of her time was spent in bed, so tired did she feel. There was to be no festivity for her, though her sons would be visiting her.

Robin had already acknowledged her gesture of thanks, but decided that Christmas morning to visit her. It was not only a mark of appreciation, but to show that he cared about her future. So, after breakfast, he went to her home, not far from the General, and took her a bottle of wine with the good wishes of the Unit.

Rachel and her husband had not expected his visit. They were overcome with joy to see him and to feel that the hospital cared for her. He was also pleased to see how well she was coping and managing the pump. She was due to visit the clinic a few days later for the necessary check-up and would be seen personally by Geoff Dalton. He too had received from her a similar card and present.

In an age when medicine was going to be made more and more impersonal by insensitive political changes, it was heartwarming to see such professional closeness between doctor and patient. The state was heading for a lack of civility towards the profession which, nonetheless, wanted to remain a servant to the community.

* * * * * * * *

Zoë turned out to be an attractive and intelligent girl, easy-going and unsophisticated. Louise was pleased when she offered her help at the dining table and later in the kitchen, though Lucille always helped her mother. The three got on well together.

The Christmas lunch was interrupted by two telephone calls. The first was for Linda, from Canada. The second was from the cruise ship, for Zoë. Rodney had given her his parents' telephone number, having asked if he could do so - nothing in that household was taken for granted. The call to Linda moved the conversation to Canada and then to the Azores, where Zoë's parents were at the time.

As expected, Cio-Cio demanded her share of attention. The

moment the children came back home she was all over them, recognising her family members very quickly, following them round and insisting on being picked up and cuddled. Being carried around draped over a shoulder was her favourite recreation. She ignored Robin almost completely. She had forgotten where his desk was, and did not sit on his lap when he watched the evening news on the television.

Sometimes, when Robin watched a football match, Cio-Cio would join him facing the TV set. It was obvious that she was following the movements of the footballers across the screen. She would, at times, sit on top of the set and bend over to be closer to the screen, a paw chasing the ball. This would cause laughter, which did not please her. Both children, and specially Lucille, had taught her to give little kisses when asked to do so. When they were children, she would butt their chins with her head when they tried to kiss her. So they trained her to kiss them instead by saying the word.

That Christmas, she was insisting more than ever on her share of attention, the more so as Zoë too had taken to her. She became so demanding as they sat down to lunch that she had to be put out through the front door and the cat-flap door closed. This did not please her.

They were in the middle of savouring their Christmas pudding when there was an unusual knock at the front door, like the postman delivering letters. Robin went to the door, but strangely enough there was no one there. No sooner had he sat down than there came another knock. This time he went to the dining-room window to investigate.

He laughed out loud. It was Cio-Cio pushing her paw in and out of the letter box to ask to be admitted. She was not going to be left out in the cold. Lucille sided with her and begged for her to be allowed in. She went to the door, picked he up and said 'Give a kiss.'

Cio-Cio was so pleased at being re-admitted that she kissed Lucille several times, to everyone's amusement. She had understood the punishment, and went and sat quietly on a chair, just being sociable.

'I think she has lost weight' Lucille remarked. 'I hope she's not having kidney problems.'

Neither Louise nor Robin had noticed her insidious loss of weight. Lucille could be right. Louise promised to get her to the vet in the New Year to have blood taken to check on her body chemistry. Lucille wanted to be informed of the results. It crossed Louise's mind that she could be diabetic.

Cio-Cio had a delightful habit of drinking from the cold tap of the kitchen sink. It was of a lever type that she could push down. Once the water trickled she would drink from the flow. However she never turned it off. This meant that occasionally the tap went on running if no one was around. Whenever no one was in, the kitchen door had to be shut. Louise had noticed that Cio-Cio was drinking more frequently. Lucille could well be right that the little feline was now having a terminal problem.

After lunch, everyone felt a little dozy. Every now and then Robin's mind would float out for a split second to Bath. But home was home. He was with all those he cherished and did not allow that corner of his emotions to intrude into a happy family occasion.

Lucille offered to play the piano. She was good at it, having reached a grade five level when at school. She knew her father's favourite tunes and after playing several of Chopin's pieces, she broke into Lara's Theme, sending Robin quietly into a day dream.

A few days later, the house was quiet again. Louise had gone out to the local sales and Robin was left with his thoughts. A new year was on him. Little had yet been solved at the General and he wondered where they would be by next Christmas.

He wrote down some of his thoughts and concerns and put them into a letter to Georgiana, so that when she went back to work between then and the New Year, she would have something from him waiting for her.

CHAPTER TWENTY

As promised to Lucille, once the New Year's festivities were over, Louise had taken Cio-Cio to the vet in the second week of January. She had come back with a small area of her right front limb shaved to expose a vein from which blood had been taken. The little creature did not look very pleased about her experience. A few days later the results were phoned through, and they left Louise and Robin shocked. Cio-Cio was in pre-terminal renal failure. Lucille's observation had been correct. Louise had noticed that the little cat was not visiting the school as frequently as she had always done, nor had she reacted to the school bell as usual, but it was winter and Louise had simply put it all down to the cold weather and the children's Christmas holidays.

The vet had suggested putting the cat on a special diet, but when it was offered to her she turned her nose up and gave Louise such a look that she felt guilty about it. When Louise reported this to Robin he laughed about Cio-Cio's reaction and agreed with the cat.

'She's over 17' Robin pointed out. 'That's a long life. What a lot of pleasure and love she has given us. I think we should let nature take its course and let her enjoy what quality of life she still has. It will be painful for us, far more than for her.'

'She seems still full of life and just as loving' Louise replied.

'Yes' said Robin, somewhat sadly. 'She'll stay that way until the very last, and then suddenly night will fall on her life.'

'Do you think I should tell the children?'

Robin hesitated for a moment. He was choosing his words.

'She is part of us all. They must not be kept in the dark. Lucille is bound to ask what the vet said.'

Louise agreed. She reflected how cats must have changed their behaviour over the years to adapt to man's own way of life and become a happy part of the human household. There must have been mutations that made this possible, she felt.

'Probably nurture played a role as well' remarked Robin.' I doubt if cats ever enjoyed marmalade on toast and curry and rice in the wild as our little one does.'

'Perhaps she was descended from an Indian tiger.'

'Yes, and perhaps women evolved from mermaids by splitting their tails to produce legs!' Robin said jokingly.

'Sounds more like a Lamarckian idea of men for their own benefit' Louise countered.

'I don't think the inheritance of acquired characteristics had much to do with it, but it's a nice thought' said Robin. 'Mermaids lured men to their demise and Calypso was a seductress.'

'I'd like one day to see a cat's genome in the same way we are now decoding the human one' she continued.

She was thinking of the project started in the States the year before to decipher man's genetic code. Robin had told her that in 1988 that he had once met James Watson, co-discoverer with Francis Crick of the double helix structure of DNA, and felt elated at the news of his appointment as head of the project the year after. Since then, there had been commercial voices wanting genes to be patented, and Watson had been opposed to this. Could this harm the project, he had wondered, and would George Bush allow such patents? The next presidential election was not due until 1992, and anything could happen meanwhile.

'The combinations and permutations of genes are the work of nature, not of man. The products of evolution should not be patented' Robin argued.

Evolution appears to be the child of convergence. Given the right environment it is nurtured to the same end product. Were our planet a few million miles nearer to the sun our vast waters could have been turned into huge swirling clouds insulating it. A similar distance further away and the seas would have been ice instead. Without rotation on an axis, there would be no day or night, while the tilt of that axis gives us the benefit of seasons. Optimal geographical and geophysical characteristics have made life as we know it possible, and the apparent hit-and-miss behaviour of evolution is not what it seems, as evolution seems always to converge to the same purpose, namely a stable outcome. Were other heavenly bodies blessed with similar characteristics, it seems more than likely that the same form of life would emerge, with similar evolutionary processes. Man would end up behaving in the same way and displaying numerous forms of intelligences, be they mental, emotional, cultural, spatial or otherwise. He would relate to other species in the same way, and they in turn would relate to him equally and be happy to become pets in his household. The personalities of these pets would tend - again through convergence - to reflect his own.

Cio-Cio, with the special mental gift of an aristocat, was displaying a social behaviour and an emotional intelligence that reflected her contact with her human surroundings. Manipulation was her favourite game, while anticipation was her greatest pastime. She had been bred to treat humans as her family, having no feline one of her own to associate with or remember, or mourn her at her passing. Somehow, to her, humans had been allowed to live with her.

Though Robin had at first accepted that Cio-Cio's time with them was limited, deep inside he felt perturbed at the thought of losing her. It was thus natural that when he rang Georgiana from his rooms on the second Wednesday of the month he had to tell her about it. She had noticed the moment he spoke to her that there was sadness in his voice, so great had become the communion between them. She soon realised why, when he informed her of his anguish. She did not forget to thank him for his end-of-the-year letter, but she too had something, somewhat on the painful side, to tell him.

'Philip has had a letter from an American drug house in California. They're trying to head-hunt him as a clinical director with a substantial salary. He is flying there tomorrow and it's more than likely he'll be offered the post. It looks as if the meeting in Bath won't happen, because by then I may well have joined him.'

Robin was taken by surprise, but diplomat that he was, he measured his words.

'That's nice for him. Congratulations. I am sure that your work with Satra will stand you well and you should be able to find something there for yourself.' He paused for a moment. 'But I shall miss you terribly.'

'So will I miss you. I'm really torn about it. I need to see you, if only to get it off my chest.'

'I understand, but your duty is to your home. Hopefully your work with Satra may bring you back sometimes. I'll always be here for you.'

It was now Georgiana's turn to be silent for a moment. They were both feeling the wrench.

'Philip won't be back till next Tuesday. Will you be able to ring me next Friday afternoon, rather than Wednesday? He'll know by then.'

Robin agreed. Now the wait would be painful for both of them, and they both showed it in their voices. It was a pain they could only share with each other.

Satra had informed Robin that they were planning a seminar in Rouen. This could be his only opportunity of being with Georgiana again, but no date had yet been fixed.

CHAPTER TWENTY ONE

True to his word, Robin rang Georgiana the following Friday, the 18th. The previous day, a coalition of some thirty-two nations, including several Arab states, had launched a massive air offensive against Iraq. The latest news was that Saddam had retaliated by raining ballistic missiles on adjoining countries as well as on Israel.

When they spoke that afternoon Georgiana had also followed the news.

'I hope there won't be a chemical retaliation by Saddam. I know you're afraid for your own hospital' she said.

'So far it's only aerial bombing, but if destruction is severe retaliation is possible. On the other hand it may knock some sense into the régime there. More importantly, what's the news on your side?'

'Philip has definitely accepted the post. I'm sorry. They want him as soon as possible.'

'Won't he have to fulfil his obligations to his present employer first?'

'Yes and no. He had told his MD before he left for California last week, and they're prepared to let him go fairly soon provided he comes back to present the results of his research at a meeting in June. His post-doctorate associates will continue with his work until there is a new appointee.'

'What will happen to your house?'

'The new company are prepared to pay to put us up in a suitable apartment for a year to help us settle. Philip thinks that in the meantime we should rent out our house in Bath, as the housing market at the moment is not very favourable. Anyway, we don't want to burn our bridges yet.'

'That makes sense.'

'There are many things I want to say to you, but preferably not on the phone. We need to meet, if you can fit it into your own timetable. I can be flexible here. The best moment will be when Philip is away, as he has to go back to California fairly soon.'

'Keep me in the picture then. My best time is always on a Wednesday, but there's also be the odd Saturday when Louise joins her artist group for the whole day.'

'Great. I'll call you ASAP. Love you.'

'Love you too.'

And with that, they said goodbye.

* * * * * * * *

January had slowly drifted into February and it was already the first Sunday of the new month. After having watched Antiques Roadshow and listened to the latest evening news bulletin, Robin retired to his desk to study the CVs of his new juniors before meeting them the next day.

The procedure for many years had been for the juniors to start their first six-month appointments after qualifying on the 1st August and move to their next six-month posts on 1st February the year after. It was a good system, as it allowed an orderly rotation without loss of time between jobs. Appointments were usually decided some months before the aspiring doctors sat for their final examinations, thus giving them a sense of security in the knowledge that they would be in employment for a year. On some clinical units, the middle strata of hospital posts also rotated on these dates.

On Robin's unit, the custom was for him to keep out of the way on these introductory days to allow his juniors to settle in. His Senior Registrar, Tom Morgan, would induct them and see that they were fully briefed for their first ward round with their chief. They had started on the Friday, and Tom had made sure that they were fully prepared for the Monday morning ward round.

Tom had been a London graduate and had won acclaim for his erudition in surgery, not only collecting two major medical school prizes in that discipline but by walking away with a first-class distinction in the subject in his finals. He had been Robin's houseman eight years previously, and now was well on the way to becoming a consultant.

He was a tall Cornishman with dark wavy hair and shining brown eyes. There was something gentle in his sharp-featured face, to which full lips added a touch of sensuality. He was a favourite among the nursing staff, particularly the operating theatre team, who always show partiality to those with dexterity. Tom excelled as a technician.

It was clear that this February entry was going to be the last of its kind. The Chairman of the group, through the Chief Executive, had all but laid down the law, but had carefully avoided upsetting Robin's unit by making some concessions which others had not been given. He had been a political appointment a year previously to implement the ill-thought-out Thatcherite 'internal market'. He supposedly knew something about business, but had moved sideways on the obvious road to a 'gong' as his company made repeated donations to the Party's fund.

Ever since the General and the North Poplar had merged into one group, the division of labour with respect to surgical emergencies had been straightforward. The General had four surgical units and the North Poplar three. It seemed sensible to split the emergency admissions equitably with the General covering four days and the North Poplar three, the two hospitals alternating their emergency 'take' at weekends. On that first weekend of February,

Robin's unit was not on duty, and this had allowed Tom to settle in the new juniors and have the weekend off.

On the Monday morning Robin was getting ready to leave for the hospital when the phone rang. Louise answered it.

'Your registrar' she called to Robin in his study.

'OK, I'll take it from here' he replied as he picked up the extension phone on his desk. It was a distraught Tom at the other end. When he heard what he had to say, Robin put his coat on and dashed out of his study.

'Is everything all right?' asked Louise.

'Geraldine has had to be rushed into hospital and Tom has to take his kids to school. He'll be late for the ward round.'

'Did he say what was the matter?'

'He was in a rush and I didn't ask, but he sounded upset. He wants to see me privately after the ward round. I don't like the sound of it.'

'Where has she been admitted?'

'The Royal Archway.'

'That's where she works.'

'Yes' replied Robin.

'Perhaps I should go and visit her.'

'Let me see first what's it's all about. If you can help, I'll call you after I've talked to Tom.' And with these words Robin rushed out.

Since Tom was going to be late, Robin felt he should get to the wards before nine o'clock to offer guidance to his house officers in preparation for the round.

It was some time after ten when Tom joined his chief, halfway through touring his first ward.

'Thank you for making the effort to join us so early' Robin said softly to him.

'Thank you sir' Tom replied, not quite knowing what else to say.

He looked pale and vacant. His eyes had a glazed appearance and he was clearly having to make an effort to concentrate.

Robin went about the two ward rounds as if they were no different from any other day, so as not to divulge anything. He respected the confidence of his juniors too much to show the slightest trace of any knowledge about their private lives. They mirrored that respect by looking upon him almost as a father figure, and he enjoyed the relationship.

Robin's team had been on emergency duty the previous Thursday, the last day of the six-month rotation period of the junior teams. As per regulations, Tom had had to sleep in that night in the duty room.

At the Royal Archway, the 'House' was having its leaving party with a riotous evening of music, dancing and drinking. Geraldine had been invited by the departing juniors of her unit. The children were left in the charge of Sylvia.

As the party got boisterous, a group of those not on duty decided to go for a splash in the hospital swimming pool. With no swimsuits at hand, the group were in their underwear, and some of the more brazen females without their bras. Alcohol had subdued all inhibition. Geraldine, usually demure, had been led astray by her juniors and had joined them in the pool in her smalls. When they went back to the dancing and drinking, she left off her wet undergarments, increasing the impressions of physical accessibility.

She had drunk more than she could hold and soon fell deeply asleep on one of the spare beds, to wake up much later and eventually find her way home. She was left with a frightful hangover and aching legs, contused, she thought by the dancing. When she crawled back to work that morning her juniors teased her about the good time she had had, but she could not remember.

That Friday evening, Tom had gone to one of the statutory

lectures at his surgical college. Sitting in the row in front were some of the surgical officers of the other hospitals. They were joking as they waited for the lecture to start, and laughing about some of their antics the evening before. Someone was goading an Australian colleague next to him.

'You bastard. You were taking advantage of her because she was drunk.'

'Man, she was a goner. She didn't mind. I reckon she enjoyed it. It was hard work, though.'

'She's married to a nice guy at the General. You should have had more respect.'

'Don't be silly, man. Geraldine wouldn't mind. She'd keep quiet about it.'

Tom suddenly realised who they were talking about and was disturbed by what he had heard. He hardly took the lecture in. Should he raise it at home, and if so, when?

He drove back in a haze. He was silent that evening after he had gone and looked at the children, as he always did, happy in their sleep. It was Sylvia's free week-end and she had gone home earlier on. He decided not to raise the subject at so late an hour.

He slept badly and woke up tired. He was again silent that Saturday morning, but Geraldine just thought he was tired from his emergency night.

It was her shopping morning, so Tom played with the children, gave them their lunch and put them to bed for their afternoon nap. When she came back, she saw how harrowed Tom looked and realised something was on his mind. It was then that he spilt the beans and told her what he had heard. It could not have been her they were talking about, protested Geraldine. She certainly didn't remember anything of that sort happening.

Geraldine then called one of her colleagues and left the house.

When she came back later she was in tears and went straight to bed, leaving Tom to deal with the children. She could not face him.

On the Sunday morning, she could not be woken up. Tom had to call Sylvia and ring for an ambulance. Geraldine was taken to her own hospital for admission.

Robin had gone back to his office after the ward round. Tom followed him a few minutes later and knocked at the door.

'Come in. Close the door Tom.' He pointed to the spare chair. 'Sit down.'

'Thank you, sir.'

'Tell me about Geraldine.'

A distraught Tom, his voice faltering and at time almost in tears, told him the full story. Geraldine had taken an overdose of Paracetamol and had needed a stomach washout. Robin had guessed that something had gone wrong, but had not expected this.

'Has she come round?' he asked.

'Yes. She's fully conscious.'

'Are her kidneys OK?'

'No damage, luckily.'

'It's been a cry for help Tom - your help. Don't stand in judgment over her. The abuser is the culprit. It's a one-off. I can't see her becoming a victim like that again. Alcohol is a wrecker. Can Louise and I help?'

Tom bowed his head, his eyes on the floor, his hands pressed together.

'I feel ashamed of what she has done. She can't face me and I am not sure I can face her. I am not even sure I can go back home.'

'Geraldine loves you' Robin said firmly. 'You are in love with her. There was no consent on her part. Some irresponsible brute took advantage of her. It's not far off rape. It wasn't the Geraldine you and I know. Don't spoil a beautiful relationship because of the impropriety of some immoral bastard.'

CHAPTER TWENTY ONE

Tom remained lost for words. Would he be able to cope?

'I want a cup of coffee' Robin said to break the silence. 'How about you?'

Tom nodded. Robin left the room for a short while and came back with two cups, by which time Tom had regained his composure.

'Let me talk to you, man to man. If the same had happened to Louise, I would not hold it against her. I love her too much. You and Geraldine are a wonderful pair. You both will have successful careers. You both have a fabulous future. If I have any advice to give you, it is not to get the law involved. Solicitors don't create reconciliation. They live from polarising people. They create revenge. Do you want retribution? If so, why?'

Tom hesitated for a moment.

'Not against Geraldine.'

'So against whom?'

Tom gave no reply.

'Do you know who the miscreant was?' And before he could answer, Robin continued. 'Probably not. If you can find out - may be from Geraldine, if at all -- let me know. I have colleagues at the Royal Archway. I shall make sure this does not happen again.'

'I still don't know how to face Geraldine' Tom said pressing his hands together.

'Is she coming home today?'

'I have to go and fetch her this afternoon. There is an abdomino-perineal resection on the list and you need my help. The two clash.'

'That's fine.' Robin already knew what his answer to that would be. 'Let me ring Louise and ask her to fetch Geraldine. I'll tell her we've had a chat about what happened. It would make matters easier when you get home and she would be there already.'

Tom looked happier. He understood the good sense of what Robin was suggesting.

'Why don't you go to the florist down the road and get her a nice bunch of roses. You don't have to say anything to her when you get home. Give her the flowers and your usual kiss. That will say it all. This is what forgiveness is about. Don't make it hard for her to seek exoneration for something she hasn't really done.'

Tom seemed to like the idea, but again could not find the right words.

'I'll ring Louise now and ask her to fetch Geraldine. She's very fond of you both. I'm sure she'll iron it out without any difficulty.'

Tom got up. His eyes were still damp. 'Thank you again, sir.'

'We like you as much as our own children. Stay that way.'

Robin extended his right hand to Tom and shook his very firmly. When Tom had gone, he rang Louise to tell her what happened.

When Tom got home, Geraldine had already picked up the children and was looking after them. She heard the front door open and rushed to it. As Tom walked in with the flowers, she hugged him. 'Thank you, darling' she said. Tom hugged her in return.

'Dad, Dad!' the children shouted as they rushed to greet him. They wanted him to see the pictures they had drawn at school that day.

It was just the happy family Robin wanted.

CHAPTER TWENTY TWO

Cio-Cio was now sleeping for much of the day and had stopped visiting the school. She was no longer responding to the bell, nor was she waiting at the front door for Robin to come back from work. Her life was gently ebbing away, and Robin was feeling it. She still loved being picked up and stroked, though she butted her head less than she had.

On the night of Thursday the 21st she looked very fragile, but she still asked to sleep between Robin and Louise in bed and would still give a little purr on being given a little kiss.

On waking up on the Friday morning, Robin found her lethargic and felt she would not last the day. Before leaving for work, he placed her gently in her basket below a radiator saying to her 'Goodbye, little love'. She opened her eyes at his voice and fixed him for a few seconds. It was almost as if she was saying 'You're going to work, see you later'. Then she closed them again. That last look of hers haunted him while driving to work.

On reaching his office he looked up the phone number of a garden nursery in Poplar where he had often bought old-fashioned varieties of rose bushes for his favourite garden. They had in stock the one he wanted to bloom over Cio-Cio's little grave. His emotions for his cherished little cat ran deep.

Robin's morning was enlivened by Rachel attending his joint out-patients session with Geoffrey Dalton. Her follow-up scan the week before had reported that the lesion had almost entirely disappeared. They were all pleased, but thought it wise for her to complete her course of chemotherapy, after which she would most probably need a small local resection. They would discuss this fully at their next multi-disciplinary clinical meeting.

For a while this good news lifted the cloud hanging over Cio-Cio, and rather than have lunch he drove instead to the nursery to collect his rose bush, a fragrant salmon-pink variety which would flower freely every year for many years to come.

He was in a hurry to get back home that evening. Under the light in the porch there was no little cat as usual. Louise opened the door for him.

'How's Cio-Cio?'

'She's still with us. She's in her basket.'

He went to the basket. 'Hello, sweetheart.'

Cio-Cio was lying stretched out on her side. She heard his voice and would have caught his scent, for she opened her eyes and made an effort to rise, but she was too weak and dropped back on to her side.

Robin picked her up and cuddled her in his right arm, his left hand feeling the soft beat of her little heart. He gave her bowed head a little kiss and held her still for a moment.

'Her heart has stopped' he said.

Her little body gave a sudden shudder. She had waited for his return before leaving the world.

Louise felt the full impact of his mortification over their loss and put her arms over his neck to join him in their sorrow.

Robin curled her little body into a ball, placed her back in her basket and covered her with her little blanket.

'I'll dig a little place for her in the rose garden' he said. Tears were trickling down his cheeks. 'I've got a rose to mark the spot.'

'A nice thought.' Louise added, 'which one?'

'Madame Butterfly.'

'Ah, yes. Cio-Cio-San.'

Robin was quiet over dinner, still torn with grief. He had expressed already how much he felt over the loss of what he called their 'third child' and now he needed to exteriorise his emotions, silently. He had to write about them to get them off his chest. After supper he quietly went to his desk overlooking his rose garden. There was no little cat sitting on his blotting pad as he wrote to Rodney and to Lucille, and then to Georgiana. He would post the letters the next morning after placing Cio-Cio in her eternal resting place. He read them to himself before closing them and addressing them, re-reading the one to his lover.

Cherished G,

Eternal slumber has now cast upon my little Cio-Cio its icy mantle of peace. She will tomorrow lie in a chosen resting place amongst roses, with a special one spreading its fragrance over her and blooming repeatedly a remembrance of the happiness and love she gave us for so long, but now free from the sorrows of this world. From the confines of my subconscious mind, I hear in the far distance the evocative lilt of Puccini's 'Un bel di', only to be reminded that she will not come back again.

A strange loneliness now inhabits her special place in my heart, for this fluffy, loving little creature meant so much, and strangely, so much more now.

No more will I see a friendly little figure standing under the porch to welcome me. No more a warm ball curled up on my knees or stopping me from writing at this desk. No more her company sitting on a chair beside me while we dine, or watching the news with me. No more shall I hear that dulcet purr of contentment, her soft expression of love. She gave back more than she was given, generously. No more her little trick of reaching the bedroom before we did with her wide deep chartreuse eyes saying 'can I stay please?'.

CHAPTER TWENTY TWO

Now only pain is left, for grief is the deepest expression of love.

'And this past life is mine no more;
The flying hours are gone,
Like transitory dreams given o'er
Whose images are kept in store
By memory alone '.

Why do we have to love so much, and how much more will I now lose?   R.

* * * * * * * * *

On the Sunday, with no Cio-Cio on his lap, Robin listened to the news that the coalition forces had launched their ground offensive to bring Saddam to his knees. His boast of a battle to end all battles was proving an empty one, and it sounded as if his forces would not hold for long.

Louise, aware of the loneliness he was feeling, came and sat with him and used the occasion to update him on her artists' forthcoming Saturdays of studies.

CHAPTER TWENTY THREE

Robin was in his office at lunch time on the Monday dealing with his correspondence of the day when his phone rang.

'Chesham' he answered.

'Are you free to speak?'

'G, how nice to hear from you.'

'I got your letter. I'm so sorry about Cio-Cio.'

'Thank you, it's kind of you to say so.'

'I had a cat when I was a child. She died in my last year at school. I cried all day. You have a need to love - perhaps you should get another cat.'

'It's too early to make decisions like that, but I'll think about it. You can never replace such a loss. I'm accepting it and adjusting to it, but it's painful.'

'I understand. I wish I could fill the gap for you.'

'So do I. How's it going?'

'Things are moving fast. Philip's flying out again on the 21st of March and he'll be away for nearly two weeks. Any chance we could meet? I have to empty the house of some of the treasured possessions we'll have to leave behind. I thought I'd take them to Henley for my parents to look after. I could do it one weekend.'

'We could definitely meet. Louise is out all day Saturday 23rd. Is that any good?'

'Sounds fine. What do you want to do?'

'We could meet for lunch, somewhere near Henley perhaps?'

'That would be perfect.'

'One of my patients runs a restaurant to the west of Windsor. I'm sure he could look after us in a private dining room. We could talk without being interrupted.'

'That would suit me well. I can drive to you that Saturday morning and take a load to Henley in the afternoon. My cousin's the manager of the Heathrow Royal, so I could leave my car there. Perhaps you could collect me from there?'

'It's a deal. I could get there by noon, or before if you like. I'll organise a nice lunch. Anything you would like?'

'I'll leave it to you. I trust your taste. I'm sure you'll choose courses we'll both enjoy.'

'Thanks. I'll call you nearer the time to fix it all. I'll be able to stay till about four.'

'That's wonderful. We have so much to talk about. Time always passes so quickly when we're together.'

When they rang off, Robin rang his restaurateur, who was only too pleased to accommodate him. They discussed the food and decided on the wines. He wanted Georgiana to enjoy the occasion; it might be their last intimate moments for a long time.

As Robin put the phone down, there came a knock at the door. 'Come in.'

It was Ian Cook. Robin invited him to sit down.

'We have a little problem with junior staffing' said Cook. 'We'd like your thoughts on the matter.'

'Surprise surprise! What's the problem?'

'The surgical officers' staffing in the new house in August leaves us short of cover for emergencies once a fortnight. We're wondering what to do about it.'

'But the job descriptions have already been publicised. When I got the ones for my team, I discussed them with Tom and we have no problem. You as Medical Director signed them with the CEO.

CHAPTER TWENTY THREE

You two would surely have worked out the roster when you did this?'

'Well, it all seemed OK at the time, but now this problem has come to light.'

'I could argue that you've both made your beds and you ought to lie in them! This is the real problem. In collaboration with the CEO you propounded policies without working out their implications properly, purely and simply to bow low to your political masters. You don't appear interested in clinical outcomes, only your own managerial aggrandisement.'

'You're being overcritical' Cook said, somewhat angrily.

'I disagree' Robin retorted. 'It's fair criticism. I said all along that cutting funds and turning the profession into a trade would damage clinical quality and endanger the system. At the present rate there won't be an NHS in ten years' time. Meanwhile standards will be eroded and we'll suffer endless litigation.'

'We did listen. We spared you the cuts. I thought you'd be helpful.'

'You spared my team because I was prepared to stand up and be counted. You were afraid of the publicity you'd get if you didn't do so. And with the stupidity of an internal market you would have lost the revenue from tertiary referrals to my Unit. So you were not doing me a favour. You were simply protecting your own backs.'

'That's stretching it. Perhaps you should not be so personal. We would appreciate your suggestions about covering the gap in the surgical roster.'

'OK. There may be two possibilities here. One, we could wait for the new intake in August and then ask if any of my juniors would be prepared to help out in turn. However, I have my doubts about that.'

'Why?'

'The juniors feel that reducing their numbers will hamper communication about patients' treatments. That would disrupt continuity of care, with mistakes being made for which they'll be blamed. I sympathise with them. For the record, will there be added remuneration for these sessions at overtime rates, if someone is prepared to help? I'd like this confirmed in writing before I broach the subject with the new entry.'

'We would have to find the extra funds. What's your other suggestion?'

'Can I just clear up one point first? You have agreed with doctrinaire policies that the NHS should now be consultant-run as opposed to consultant-led. Am I right?'

'Well, yes.'

'Then I suggest the cover you require should be given by the consultants involved. This would be in keeping with the agreement while at the same time protecting the juniors' job descriptions. This seems a fairer solution.'

Ian Cook had not expected this and felt torpedoed. He had no answer to it. After a painful silence, all he could say was that he would raise the matter with the other consultants before taking it to the CEO.

'Good luck' said Robin, keeping a straight face. 'Keep me in the picture.'

Senseless medical politicians had brought this on the system. They had put personal interest before clinical outcome, unlike their more dedicated colleagues. Would they, so late in their game, be able to solve this self-created impasse?

CHAPTER TWENTY FOUR

As the last day of February gave way to the first one of March, the large-scale ground offensive in Iraq was achieving victory. There was no longer any fear that the General would have to cope with casualties from the war zone. During the ensuing week the terms of surrender emerged - Saddam must destroy his nuclear, biological and chemical weapons programme and a UNO trade embargo would be imposed.

Not everyone was happy about such lenient terms. There was criticism of the Bush administration choosing to allow Saddam to remain in power rather than pushing on to capture the Iraqi capital and overthrow the dictator and his government. It was argued that such an aggressive policy would split the coalition alliance as some Arab states saw an intact Iraq as an important bulwark against Iranian hegemony. Furthermore, many in the States felt that if the coalition forces had occupied Baghdad and had the task of running the country, they could find themselves there for many years to come, not to mention unnecessary casualties.

For the Kurds and the southern Shi'ites this was bad news. They realised that the coalition forces were not liberating them from Saddam and they could sense brutal treatment in the years to come. Yasser Arafat, who had overtly supported Saddam, was now silent, more so knowing that several thousand PLO supporters in the region would undoubtedly be expelled. Reflective historians, however, felt that further problems would rock Mesopotamia in years to come with perhaps another local hostility inevitable.

The General might have avoided the possibility of receiving war casualties, but Ian Cook as Medical Director was now suffering a new headache in addition to the one his discussion with Robin Chesham had given him. Five days previously, under his emergency cover, a 17-year-old boy, Keith Hall, had been admitted following a severe head injury. He had been forbidden by his parents from riding as a pillion passenger on the back of his friend's motorbike. His parents had thought the friend a fairly wild boy racer and feared the worst if they had an accident.

While driving recklessly downhill, the friend had had to brake suddenly to avoid hitting an elderly lady crossing the road. As a result, Keith was catapulted forward, hitting the road head first. He was brought unconscious to the General, breathing with difficulty and having to be kept alive on a ventilator. By the third day he was showing no response to pain or temperature and no visual reaction to light, his pupils remaining fixed. He was pronounced brain dead, not being able to be weaned off the ventilator.

There was a religious problem. Keith had been baptised a Catholic, his mother being of that faith. The father was a non-conformist. Discussions about switching off the ventilator met with refusal from the mother. It fell to Ian Cook to talk to the parents.

'I am not prepared for him to be destroyed' said Mrs Hall vehemently. 'God gave him life and God's will must prevail.'

'But, Mrs Hall, his brain is no longer able to function and we are keeping him alive artificially. He cannot breathe on his own' said Cook.

'I know, but his heart's still beating, so he's still alive' said Mrs Hall.

'That's only because we are keeping him breathing with a machine' Cook explained. 'The moment we stop giving his heart oxygen it will stop.'

It was stalemate, not helped by the CEO (whose nickname was now Il Duce), who had implied that supporting a purposeless life artificially was a major demand on the hospital's finances. He was there to take decisions. It amounted to formulaic bureaucracy by someone with neither clinical judgment nor an understanding of the emotional pain the parents were suffering. His attitude soon leaked out to the nursing and medical staff, who both vocalised strong objections.

'I appreciate the medical arguments about switching off the ventilator' said Mr Hall. 'But if I stand in the way of my wife's beliefs it will make life even more difficult, if that's possible.'

This point was fully accepted by Keith's medical attendants, but they sensibly pointed out that the inevitable would take place and postponing it would not change the situation.

'What are the chances of Keith eventually breathing on his own?' asked the father.

'Virtually nil' said Cook.

'Could it be tried longer as a compromise? It might allow my wife to come to terms with the inevitable.'

'I am sure we can do that. How long do you want us to try?' asked Ian Cook.

Mr Hall quite naturally found this difficult to answer and simply begged time to put it to his wife and come to a decision. The delay helped Cook, as he could refer it to the Hospital Ethics Committee or even seek legal advice if need be. He therefore agreed to see Mr Hall two days later.

When Ian Cook had chosen to take on the role of Medical Director, he had never thought that such a problem would land in his lap. Now he found himself with a responsibility he had not envisaged.

However awkward Ian Cook found Robin Chesham, he nonetheless respected the latter's judgment and clear-sightedness, and decided to ask him for his opinion. He knew that Robin had set up the Hospital Ethics Committee eight years previously, following the various Articles of the Human Convention. Robin had heard about Keith Hall's near-fatal injury as well as the CEO's views. Cook explained the problem to him.

'A very sad situation' agreed Robin. 'As you know I am a humanist, but I understand fully the damage that indoctrination can cause. This is a harrowing clinical problem. It is neither an administrative nor a religious one. The CEO shouldn't interfere unless it has to go to court. I gather your social worker thinks she should be involved. I would strongly advise against this, as she is overtly Opus Dei.'

'Yes, we know that. We have no intention of discussing it with her.'

'The cardinal point here is that death is no longer a natural event but a process under clinical determination. There is a compassionate need to soothe Mrs Hall and try to allay her enormous grief. I feel for her. Have you thought of pointing out to her that it could be a divine intention for her son to die in order to save other lives?'

This had not crossed Ian Cook's mind. 'Do you mean organ donation?'

'Yes. To her, if it is God's will, it means Paradise for the boy.'

Ian Cook had to smile at Robin's percipience.

'I knew you'd work·out an answer' he said, tongue in cheek. 'If she accepts this, where do we go from here?'

'Donation must not cause distress to the family. We have to act differently from donation after cardiac arrest, because we'd take the organs before death.'

'You're right. We haven't had to face such a problem in ICU before. We are still learning.'

'I suggest you talk to our Specialist Nurse on the Transplant Team. She is first class and she's the best person to talk to the family. She is what I call a 'proper' nurse, not a university graduate who has not been trained in compassion at the bedside. She's also good at talking to the retrieval teams of recipient hospitals. It's their teams that have to decide on the suitability of any donated organ.'

'I can alert our own renal unit. The team there would move in quickly. What about other organs?'

'Well, the most needed and rarest is still a heart-lung one. Prolonged ventilation can damage lungs, but in this instance it may not be the case. It would be sensible to alert the recipient hospitals soon. As I'm sure you know, you get the best results when transplant surgery is done within four hours. So talk to our most local hospitals.'

'Which ones do you suggest?'

'The Royal Brompton is the nearest, then Harefield. If neither has a suitable recipient, then alert Papworth in Cambridge. Their helicopter team will act very promptly. They probably all hold a list of suitable candidates.'

'What about liver donation?'

'Split donation is becoming a very sensible way of maximising use. The larger portion can go to The Royal Free or The Royal London. Great Ormond Street would be only too pleased to be offered the smaller part.'

'That's very helpful. I now have a plateful. But I still have to help poor Mrs Hall come to terms with it.'

'Not an easy task. Do enlist the transplant nurse. She is better than any of us. Good luck.'

Robin patted him on the back. Time was not on Cook's side.

CHAPTER TWENTY FIVE

In the twenty-five or more years since Robin had qualified, medicine had changed beyond recognition. It was a pace of change no different from what was happening to the landscape of the nation or the architecture of its cities, or indeed the political map of Europe. Motorways had sliced their way through its green countryside; low offices had been replaced by tall skyscrapers of differing shapes; cars congested the centres of towns, while the railway system still belonged to an age past and was waiting to be fully electrified. The year before, the Berlin Wall had fallen and the autocratic régimes in Eastern Europe were heading for democracy and a more open society. The Soviet Union too was heading for decentralisation and the breaking up of its federal makeup.

In medicine, high technology was making diagnosis more precise and replacing the knife. The great advances in optics, particularly fibre optics, allowed the confines of the body to be accessed with ease, permitting physicians and radiologists to invade fields once the prerogative of surgeons. But by far the greatest advance was in the replacement of failing vital organs with transplanted normally-functioning ones.

The first kidney transplants had taken place between identical twins - same genes and thus no rejection - in 1954 in Paris and Boston. In the latter city, at Brigham Hospital, Joseph Murray carried out a very successful operation and in this present year his name was going forward for a Nobel Prize in Medicine. Since that first transplant, anti-rejection drugs had been evolved which allowed transplantation between non-related subjects, and better still those harvested at death. But the world-breaking event had been that of a heart transplant in December 1967 in Cape Town by Christiaan Barnard, which had put the case of transplantation firmly on the map and opened up the field of medicine and surgery beyond all expectations. As anticipated, there was the usual outcry by churches and creationists about man playing God, but as the procedure became more and more successful, the world started to take a more rational view.

There is no greater gift of life than the donation of a vital organ. The dead or the dying could now contribute to the welfare of the living by gifting their body to others in their will.

Stephanie, the Specialist Nurse on the Transplant Team, had been trained before her School of Nursing had been separated from the Hospital. She was taught her patient care by the bedside and not from the computers in the ward's offices. She was no clipboard nurse. Project 2000, drowned in paperwork and box ticking, had not influenced her. She could therefore talk as a human being to another human being. This was why Robin had advised Ian Cook to seek her help in coping with Mrs Hall's anguish.

She also realised that religion had always stood in the way of scientific advancement. She had dealt with the local Muslim community, which was still under the influence of the defunct Ottoman empire's rejection of progressive knowledge - hence the fact that Western concepts had not reached the minds of most successive generations. She had also interviewed several orthodox members of the Jewish community in the area and understood their difficulties with respect to organ donation.

Her open mind made her a star in the world of transplant. She had thus come to realise that the three monotheist religions - Christianity, Judaism and Islam - had much in common, but that

Christianity had used icons and art to influence unduly the illiterates of centuries past by creating images of saints and pictures of heaven, giving a sense of reality to the fantasy of religion. Judaism and Islam were simpler beliefs in direct communication with their God, and this made interviews easier for her.

At Ian Cook's insistence, Stephanie saw Mr Hall on his own when he visited his son in ICU, as he did every day after work. She found him a very balanced person with whom she had no difficulty in tête-à-tête communication. She then reported to the Medical Director.

'I've had a most enlightening interview with Mr Hall' she said. 'His son had apparently always held that if anything fatal ever happened to him he would like his various organs donated.'

'Wow! What a boon. I'm so relieved. This will make my job a lot easier. I'm grateful to you.'

'He understood our difficulties and realised that his son had only a mechanically-supported life. None of his own. He wanted a little time to slowly bring his wife round to accepting the inexorable outcome. He felt that she would eventually consent to the medical decision, but he needed to break the question of organ donation to her gently, though she would have been aware of her boy's wishes. I have asked him to ring me personally when they have reached a decision.'

'Good work, Stephanie.'

'I have also explained to Mr Hall that though I raised with him the possible question of organ donation, he won't be officially approached unless and until the decision to withdraw life-sustaining treatment has been reached. This could not be decided by the team looking after the boy but by two independent and uninvolved clinicians who had verified that further life supporting means were no longer in the patient's best interest. He understood this.'

'You've been exceptionally helpful' said Cook. 'Is there anything more we need do?'

'No, but for good measure I'll check the organ donor register and speak off the record to my opposite numbers in other transplant units. If you agree, I could have a quiet word with the Catholic priest serving the hospital about any request for last offices, though Mrs Hall may want this carried out by her own priest.'

'That's a good idea. I'm happy to leave it in your capable hands.'

Stephanie's excellent work had disburdened Ian Cook, and he was able to meet the Ethics Committee and the CEO with positive news.

Once all statutory procedures had taken place, mother and father were seen again. It was not without pain to them both, but the suggestion of donation gave quality to the boy's departure from this world. The question of tissue matching was also carefully explained to them, after which the recipients for liver, kidneys and a heart-lung preparation would be approached. The priest and members of the family were treated with utmost deference and civility as the time drew near to switching off the machine, after the various organs would have been harvested. A helicopter was waiting on the hospital pad to fly those cooled vital parts which were not to be transplanted at the General.

Later, as a mark of appreciation to the family, money was collected from many sources to subscribe to a bench with a plaque in memory of Keith to be placed in the hospital forecourt. It all helped to soften the pain felt by the family, as well as the guilt Keith's friend was suffering, for which he was offered counselling.

Keith's organ donation was the greatest gift a human being could have offered to another - of one past life to another's future one.

CHAPTER TWENTY SIX

It was Saturday the 23rd of March and Robin's Toyota was purring swiftly along the M4 as he drove to the Heathrow Royal, as agreed, to meet Georgiana. He had planned his morning so as to be there before noon, well ahead of her. When he arrived just after a quarter to twelve, he found nevertheless that she had got there first. She was waiting patiently on the steps of the hotel. As his car passed the barrier at the gate, he saw her beaming smile of welcome.

She was wearing the same elegant dress she had worn the evening they had been to the opera in Helsinki. She knew the memory of that night would cheer him, as it had remained dear to him.

'You look as lovely now as you did when I first saw you' he said as she jumped into the passenger's seat. 'And you've beaten me to it!'

'I've been impatient all week for this moment.' She leaned over and kissed him, and her passion was bordering on grief.

'It's a little early for lunch' he said. 'We can eat any time after one. We could take time over an apéritif, unless you'd prefer a walk along the river?'

'That would be nice. It's a lovely sunny day for March.'

'Let's drive to this side of the river and meander down the Thames Path until it's time to go to Bray' he suggested.

Robin took the A4 to join the motorway at junction 5, exiting two junctions later. Just before reaching the Thames bridge to Maidenhead he turned south to drive parallel to the river until they reached the Thames Path and parked short of it. With his usual politeness he went round to her side to open the door for her. When would he do this again, he thought to himself.

They walked along the river hand in hand, talking about the past and the future.

'Philip rang me last night' she said. 'He's been to the flat the company has rented for us. It's very spacious. It has a nice study with all the terminal facilities for his computer and a direct link to his new office. He can move in next week. He's suggesting I try to join him by the end of next month if Ken's OK about it.'

'I'll miss you hugely' he replied. 'Maybe I could see you off when you fly out. Didier is also leaving towards the end of next month, probably on the 28th, which is a Saturday. He's staying with us the night before, so I offered to drive him to Heathrow to catch his plane to Paris. It's the end of his sabbatical year.'

'Maybe I could arrange to leave the same day so that we could be together after Didier's departure. I've got time to plan it.'

'That's a good idea. Didier will probably catch a mid-afternoon plane to avoid the midday congestion to Paris. He's staying there with a brother of his before going to Rouen on the Monday.'

'I think there's a plane to New York as well as to LA at about seven in the evening, so that could be just right for me.'

'Well, work on it if possible. I'll be able to tell you all about Didier then. He wants to discuss the Satra May meeting in Rouen. They have asked him to organise it.'

'Pity I'll miss this' she said sadly. 'I so wanted to see Giverny with you.'

'I know. You would have enjoyed Monet's home and garden. I would have wanted you to see the cathedral of Rouen and see it as Monet painted it, in the sun and in the shade. It's been beautifully restored since it was so badly damaged in the war. You'd have liked the ambulatory. They say the heart of Charles the Fifth is buried there, as well as Richard the Lionheart's. And I could have taken you to Gill, my favourite Michelin-starred restaurant on the Quay.'

'Stop it, you're making it worse' said Georgiana. 'But I will come back to England as often as I can. Maybe we could organise a pretend visit to Giverny.'

'That's a lovely idea. I can picture you in my mind standing on that Japanese curved bridge. It's like a suspended altar in a cathedral of trees. At that time of year the white wisterias will be out. They hang their garlands over the water just like candelabras. The flowers are wonderful. I hope I can show them to you one day.'

'Maybe I could come back at the same time next year and we could go there.'

'Maybe'. Robin was dreaming of the reflection of the pendulous branches of the willow trees in Monet's lake, with the sun's rays finding a path between the slender leaves and casting simmering spots of light on the water. He thought of the Thames at Sonning. He could almost see her walking across that Japanese bridge with the dress she was wearing now contrasting against the dark screen of trees on the far side of the pond.

Georgiana saw him then as she had first seen him in a reverie, standing in front of the Sibelius Monument in Helsinki. She suffered a moment of heartache.

'It's a pity we didn't meet earlier in life' she murmured sadly.

'Love doesn't work that way' he replied very softly. 'My first love was as profound as the one I have for you. It didn't work, and I love you as much as I did her then. I still don't know why I love you in the same sort of way. Perhaps because, as the French say, 'on revient toujours à ses premières amours'. Perhaps because we live a false version of reality and are less in control of our emotions and our decisions than we care to think. We so often see the world through the eyes of those we love and have loved. The present is always patterned by the past'.

'I don't know why we want each other so much. Maybe we came

from twin stars. I'm in my seventh heaven when we make love. You have taught me to appreciate pleasure more deeply.'

'Has it disturbed you?'

'No. Quite the opposite. As I said before, it's made me reassess my relationship with Philip. It has enhanced it. I was determined, little by little, to introduce to it what I had learnt. Far from feeling guilt, it moved me away from a conventional past, as you said once. I'm grateful for that, but it has made me crave you more.'

'How nice to hear you say that without regret. I enjoy the intensity of our love. I think it would be just as intense even if we were together every day. I can't always find the right words to express my feelings. I find it easier to show them physically.'

She stopped walking and turned towards him, her wide blue-green eyes almost lost in a dream, and sneezed.

'Kiss me' she said.

After a few moments they started their walk again and ambled along in a leisurely fashion until they reached a bend of the river from which, across the water, they could see the roof of the Waterside Inn. It was time to turn back.

The restaurateur was delighted to see his surgeon again. He took them to a cosy garden room opening off a short corridor from the main restaurant. A small table had been specially prepared for them. A single red rose stood in a mini-fluted vase in the middle, flanked by baccara glasses for white and red wine. The cutlery and crockery were impeccable. Pink champagne was offered them with the restaurateur's compliments. Georgiana looked at Robin with moist eyes.

'You never stop spoiling me.'

'I don't know when I'm going to get another chance.'

'Don't worry. I'll find good reasons to come back as often as possible.'

The restaurateur reappeared to tell her what he had prepared for the occasion and what wines he would serve. There would be queues de langoustines with homard poêlé, to be washed down with a sumptuous Meursault. Duck would be the main course, with a full-bodied Shiraz. The restaurant's dessert speciality was millefeuilles in various flavours. Georgiana chose chocolate and was advised to have a glass of Maury to complement it. Robin preferred vanilla, with a pure chardonnay champagne - a 'blanc de blancs'.

Over the meal they talked of past enjoyments and what Georgiana would do in California. They sipped several cups of rich coffee and ate several petits fours. They wanted time to stand still. They wanted to savour the privacy they had been so generously offered.

When Robin asked for the bill, the restaurateur insisted that the lunch was with his compliments.

'I owe this man my life' he said to Georgiana. 'There is no price for this.'

A fitting compliment, Georgiana thought, for this last occasion.

She had decided to fly out on the same day as Didier, and to ask her mother to take her to the airport as her father would be in business in New York that week. So she could plan the day as she wished.

As Robin left her at the hotel, she kissed him again.

'Whatever the future has in store, remember I shall always love you' she said. 'Your passion towards me has made you dearest of all.'

'I feel the same way' said Robin.

CHAPTER TWENTY SEVEN

It was the last Friday in April, and they were waiting on a windy platform for the arrival of the 3.15 train to King's Cross, due there at 5.30. Bob Hirst was seeing Didier off after his year in Bob's unit. It had been a successful sabbatical for Didier, and he was now returning home. They would meet again in Rouen, so it was a short adieu.

By 5.30, Robin was already at King's Cross Station to meet Didier. Didier's heavy suitcase would remain in the car until he left, while he took his overnight attaché case into the house. On arrival at the Chesham home he was pleased to see Louise again and gave her a big hug. Observant as always, with immaculate politeness, he missed Cio-Cio's usual front door welcome and asked where she was.

Over the apéritif and Louise's delicious dinner, Didier discussed his preparations for Satra's Rouen meeting and when he said he would like Georgiana as a speaker, Robin warned him that she may not be able to join them.

'Her husband has been head-hunted by a Californian company' said Robin. 'Georgiana is joining him soon, so her work on Satra's project is likely to be interrupted, at least for the time being.'

'What a pity' commented Didier. Then looking at Louise he continued 'You know, she's one of our star lecturers, not to mention her charisma.'

'I'll second that' Robin added.

'We all like her' continued Didier. 'She is very gregarious and affable. It looks as if I may have to fall back on Ken.'

'Have I met her?' Louise asked.

'I doubt it' Robin added. 'You met Ken at the Digestive Foundation evening event a year ago, but I am not sure whether she was there that evening.'

Suddenly a thought struck Robin. Had he in fact met Georgiana that evening? Was it there that he had seen the face and heard the voice, even perhaps the giggle. That would be why he seemed to recollect so much about her. Perhaps he would yet solve the riddle, right at the end of their relationship.

He returned to their discussion and offered Didier a vintage port, which the Frenchman enjoyed until it was time for him to retire. Robin had agreed to drive him the next day to Guy's Hospital to meet the mutual colleague with whom he would be having lunch. He would collect him from there to afterwards go to Heathrow.

* * * * * * * * *

'You were moaning and groaning most of the night' Louise told her husband as he woke up. Robin had not been aware of being so noisy, but he had certainly had a restless night, frequently changing position to relieve an ache in his left shoulder. He could not remember having strained it the day before, but by the morning it felt better. Perhaps his nocturnal restlessness was just symptomatic of his sorrow at losing her.

She had rung him a few days before to say that she would be stopping in New York overnight before leaving the next afternoon for California, as her father was on business in the city and would be meeting her at JFK Airport. She would be staying with him that night.

She had stayed her final week in England in Henley with her mother. She was catching the 6.30, reaching New York soon after ten o'clock local time. The plan was for her mother to see her off at Heathrow, but she had twisted her knee the week before and could not drive. A friend of hers had offered to drop Georgiana at the airport, but her mother would accompany them. Robin had collected Didier after lunch. His plane to Paris was leaving at 4.30 from Terminus 1. Robin had arranged to meet Georgiana at Terminal 4 at 3.30, which would give them some time together.

He had arrived in very good time to park his car and had found a good vantage point from which he could watch her being dropped at the departure level. He knew that her obsession for promptness would get her there early, so he was keen to arrive first.

As he was waiting he noticed a red Ford Fiesta looking for a gap to stop and recognised Georgiana in the back of the car. It stopped some ten yards further up. He watched her mother and her friend as they came out of the car to hug G adieu. As he looked more carefully he saw what a clone of her mother she looked.

Then something struck him. He looked again, harder. He studied the hair, the eyes, the face, the way the head was held.

There was no doubt about it. He was looking at the girl he had loved and lost all those years before: Anthea.

He thought for a moment that he was hallucinating. His whole past flashed through his mind. Had he fallen in love twice with the same genes? Was Anthea right when she thought that his strong personality could leave imprints of him on her progeny?

Was there in Georgiana - and indeed in her mother - an element of himself? Was his love for Georgiana genetic, as well as epigenetic? Had he been in love only once in his life? A myriad thoughts blazed across his mind. How could he ever see Georgiana and make love to her again?

The car drove away, and as Georgiana turned round she saw him and came to him.

'You look pale, are you all right?' she said.

'Yes. It's just a sad moment' was all he could say.

After she had checked in, they went to the bar for a drink and a farewell talk.

Robin reminded her that her first letter to his rooms should be very informal, just letting him know how the journey had been and giving him an address at which she could be contacted.

'I watched your goodbyes outside the car' he said. 'I didn't have to guess which woman was your mother.'

'Everybody says I'm her spitting image.'

But Robin needed to make sure it really was Anthea he had seen. He went recklessly on.

'You never told me much about your mother except that she worked for a recruitment agency. Do you have uncles and aunts on her side?'

'No. She was an only child. Just like me.'

This was useful information. But he still needed to know her maiden name.

'How strange that I have to wait for a parting moment to find out more about your past. It seems funny that after having known you for so many months I had never thought of asking you your parents' names.'

'It's something I suppose you don't think of asking' she replied. 'My father's name is Henry and my mother is Sonia, but all her school friends call her Sam, from the initials of her maiden name.'

Robin's heart thumped. It was Anthea. He realised with a jolt that he had never stopped loving her. After all those years of bottling it up, he had fallen in love all over again with her - by meeting her daughter.

They talked of other things, but his mind was far away. He had a strange feeling of certainty that he would never be able to see her again. For if he did, how would he feel about making love to her again?

His mind was in a fog. He was certain he could never stop loving Georgiana, and he was now haunted by a premonition that this would be their last encounter, their final farewell.

A coffin of buried memories burst open. Months and years sped past like a speeded up film. Genes had twice triggered the same love. Mother and daughter were one love, one force in his life.

He was feeling unwell, but he could see she was becoming restless with her usual fear of missing her flight.

'Let me walk to you the gate' he said.

'Always the gentleman!' She took his arm.

'I shall always love you. Perhaps one day I might be able to tell you why.'

'I will love you too, forever.' There was a sad finality in her tone, a resignation, perhaps, to a future without him. Did she share his feeling that they would never see each other again?

As he gave her a last kiss at the departure gate, his eyes filled with tears. He turned away quickly from her so that she would not see him cry.

She turned and marched briskly through the gate, anxious as always to board her plane without delay. She did not see how unsteady Robin's walk suddenly became as he headed for the down escalator. All his poise and confidence had melted away. He felt he had loved and lost, not once but twice, all at the same time and all in the same dreadful, beautiful adventure. His genes and her genes had determined his fate.

The lights of the departure hall suddenly seemed unbearably bright, the air stifling, the floor unsteady, as if he had boarded a ship and sailed into hostile waters. He did not seem to be able to catch his breath. A young woman with bright red hair moved towards him to offer a hand in concern, but he brushed it away. He was fine. He needed to get home, have a drink, find some normality. As soon as the dizziness stopped he stepped on to the escalator.

* * * * * * * * *

On the way to the hospital, the paramedics in the ambulance made enormous efforts to resuscitate Robin, without success. Recognising him, one of them called their HQ to ask them to get the police to contact Robin's wife as a matter of urgency.

'Mrs Chesham?'

'Speaking. Who is this?'

'Can you confirm that Mr Robin Chesham is your husband?'

'Yes. What is this about?'

'It's Ashford Hospital. I'm afraid there's been an accident.'

'Oh my god! Is he all right?'

'Unfortunately it's quite serious, Mrs Chesham. A police officer is on his way to speak to you to explain what has happened. They'll be with you very shortly.'

By the time Louise got to the hospital Robin's death had already been certified, though the cause remained obscure until the coroner completed his post-mortem report. It revealed that he had suffered a cardiac infarct - a heart attack – the previous night. His fate had been genetically determined, of course, like that of his father and his brother before him.

At the inquest, a tearful young woman with red hair was able to describe how she had watched an elegant middle-aged man with sad, distant eyes pitch over at the top of the down escalator and fall his length to the bottom.

* * * * * * * * *

Anthea would have no reason to notice Robin's many glowing obituaries, but Georgiana, who learned the news in a letter from Margaret, would be adding them to her most cherished treasures. She would re-read them down the years, never knowing the truth, never suspecting what had made him become so suddenly and strangely thoughtful during their last moments together.

Robin had written a memorandum of his wishes, stating that, subject to the season and the wishes of his family, any celebration of his life should take place on or as near to the 11th August as possible. The music should be Lara's Theme and the love duet from Verdi's Un Ballo in Masquera. He also made special requests about where his ashes should be scattered. Some of this would make sense, but one was his most buried secret. He had told Margaret that he was to be cremated privately and that some of his ashes should be scattered on his rose garden, remembering Cio-Cio and his happy home life, and some on the Thames at Sonning. A celebration of his life and work was fixed for Saturday 10th August 1991. Georgiana knew what it all meant; his tribute to their love. She had to be there.

The celebration was held in the Great Hall of the Medical School. The love duet from Un Ballo in Masquera was the opening music. Didier, Lars Nordin and Gustav Borg attended, as did many from the Satra group, including its Medical Director. Hospital staff who were not on duty crowded into the place, as did many of his patients, including Rachel Hudson and her father.

The eulogy was given by the Dean of the Medical School, who told the gathering that a ward at the hospital was to carry his name. This met with a rapturous ovation.

Many of Robin's past registrars had travelled from their own hospitals to be there. Tom had arranged for some of them to give short papers on the research work they had carried out under him, while he himself would give an account of his latest work. These registrars were his academic progeny, and he had treated them as his children. Their work with him had set them up on the road to consultancy and he had imprinted on them his vision of medicine.

Rodney and Lucille also gave their personal appreciation of their father. They spoke of his broad-minded views and the liberalising influence he had had on their lives, respecting their wishes, sharpening their thinking and giving them a freedom their peers did not enjoy. Rodney told the audience how much his father loved Christina Rosetti's poems for the openness of her emotions, and recited one of his most loved poems, appropriate to the occasion, with the impassion his father would have shown:

Remember me when I am gone away,
Gone far away into the silent land ;
When you can no more hold me by the hand,
Nor I half turn to go, yet turning stay.
Remember me when no more day by day
You tell me of our future that you planned:
Only remember me; you understand
It will be late to counsel then or pray.

Yet if you should forget me for a while
And afterwards remember, do not grieve:
For if darkness and corruption leave
A vestige of the thoughts that once I had,
Better by far you should forget and smile
Than that you should remember and be sad.

There did not seem to be a dry eye in the room. To relieve the sadness, Lucille went to the piano and played Lara's Theme, explaining that it had been a favourite of her father's.

Louise was not dressed in black. This would have been contrary to Robin's temperament. It was after all a celebration. Georgiana had never met her, nor seen photographs of her, but she recognised her instinctively. She was wearing a bright flowery dress, and Georgiana could not help seeing something of Robin in the way she spoke and smiled.

She went up to Louise and the two children to proffer her condolences.

'I am delighted to meet you' Louise said, kissing her on both cheeks. 'Robin and Didier talked about you the evening before his death. So I am glad to know now who you are. How good of you to have come from such a long way.'

'We were all very fond of Robin. We shall miss him terribly' she replied, expressing her own feelings. She did not want to say any more for fear of bursting into tears, but she was glad to hear what Louise said and to have met her. She did not feel like a rival; just the very sort of person Robin would undoubtedly have loved.

In a corner of the hall, to the right of the podium, stood a table with many photographs of Robin at different ages. There was one taken in Helsinki on the Saturday afternoon after the conference was over. Gustav had sent Georgiana the same one. Consciously or by accident, she was standing next to Robin. He would have cherished this. There was also one of him lecturing in Paris at the Satra meeting, sent him by Didier.

Another, taken in Oxford, in the University sports ground, showed him in his college football shirt, probably taken before a match. If Georgiana had looked just a little more closely, she might have seen that in the group of attending girl friends was... her own mother.

As the celebration drew to an end she went to Louise again to say goodbye. She learned that Tom had been selected to replace Robin, exactly as he would have wished.

On her way back to Henley, she stopped at the French Horn and crossed over to the spot where she and Robin had once stood. As she stood by the edge of the river, she could picture his reflection in the water, hear the soft tones of his voice and feel the immensity of his love. The river seemed more tranquil and crystalline than ever; a river that had once brought him joy by showing him the beauty of her reflected face.

To join his ashes, she cast into the water a red rose she had bought on the way. With it she felt she was parting with a piece of her heart; the piece that had belonged to him. She stood in contemplation for a moment before drying her eyes and departing leaving behind an emotional vacuum she knew nothing would ever fill.

She was not to know that her genes had brought her to him. Genes he had fallen in love with, for ever. Would she in turn pass on to her progeny molecular parcels of their shared genes?

A year later, Georgiana returned to England to have her firstborn child on British soil. It was a boy, and she named him Robin. He would be her very own secret, and her special way of filling a void. Above all it was a homage to the memory of a love which had been short but profound, endearing, undemanding and without explanation - at least to her. It was a love she had been missing for over a year, and would go on missing for the rest of her life.

Could it be that her child would carry some of the genes she might, through her birth and by destiny, have shared with Robin? She had given the boy his name. Would he too inherit some of these shared genes of love? Had Anthea after all been right?

* * * * * * * *

ND - #0490 - 270225 - C0 - 234/156/18 - PB - 9781908223753 - Matt Lamination